SAGITTARIUS CHARMED

ZODIAC GUARDIANS 7

TAMAR SLOAN
TRICIA BARR

CONTENTS

SHREYA

"What a beautiful day," Shreya sing-songs to herself as she strolls down the quaint suburban sidewalks of Mirror Point.

When her parents first told her they were moving to New York for an extended period of time, she'd expected the Big Apple and had been looking forward to exploring. But, as she and her parents had been traveling so much for work for so long, they'd decided to settle in a less "toxic" environment and had rented a house in the suburbs instead.

Shreya can't say she minds, though. It's nice to be in a place with such a small-town vibe for once, where the city is only a bus or train ride away. And the day truly is lovely. Birds are chirping a merry tune, and there's not a cloud in the sky. Perfect conditions for wandering what she hopes will be her new stomping grounds.

A desire for something cold and sweet nibbles at her belly, and she decides to follow that sensation around a corner, which has apparently led her to the main street of town. No doubt she can find something to satisfy her craving on this road.

I always manage to find exactly what I'm looking for, she thinks. *Or rather, it usually finds me...*

Before the thought has even finished, a sign above a cute little white building grabs her attention, reading "Creamy Dreams", with the embossed picture of a cup of something swirled topped with a cherry.

I hope it's not soft-served. But then again, I'll take it either way.

She skips a little faster to her new destination, smiling when she sees people her age gathered at the tables out front. Her parents hadn't yet finished enrolling her in the local high school, and she's excited to learn if any of these teens might be in some of her classes when she starts next week.

"Hi, guys," she waves at a lively group as she approaches before hanging her thumbs on the belt loops of her favorite pair of frayed holey jeans.

The group all turn their heads toward her, frowning as they take in her edgy appearance, complete with pixie cut, spike, blond-tipped hair and a studded Rebel Saints t-shirt. She doesn't take offense at their skeptical examinations, though. She's certain they'll be her best friends soon enough.

"What's good here?" she asks in her signature chipper voice, offering them a friendly smile.

One of the guy's expressions turns from a frown to a look of appreciation, and he places himself at the head of the group.

"That depends," he begins with a somewhat goofy grin. "Do you like sweet or salty?"

"Give it up, Zach." A petite Asian girl smacks him on the shoulder. "I'm sure she's not interested."

The gorgeous blond girl perched on the corner of the tabletop scoffs and flicks a wavy lock of golden hair over her shoulder. "In his defense, is anyone? The boy's gotta cast his net as far and wide as he can." She giggles, then turns a welcoming but slightly assessing smile to Shreya. "You can't go wrong with a Caramel Banana Blast. It's the perfect mixture of both salty and sweet." She winks, thick golden lashes caressing her flawless cheek as she does so, and Shreya's certain she'll like this girl.

"Sounds perfect," she says with a grateful nod. "Maybe I'll see you around."

The blond doesn't respond, but the boy named Zach calls, "You can count on it," as Shreya pulls open the glass door and walks inside.

The inside is mostly white, with giant pictures of various fruits painted on the walls in vibrant colors. Along the back wall is a buffet-style counter displaying the multitude of toppings available in front of a large machine with a dozen or so push-down dispensers.

A wide grin spreads across her face as she realizes this establishment indeed doesn't offer soft-serve ice cream but frozen yogurt. *Yay!* How is she always so lucky to find these little hidden gems?

She approaches the counter where a pretty girl with long brown hair pulled into a ponytail is waiting to take her order.

"What can I get you?" the girl asks, and Shreya notes the name tag pinned to her shirt that reads "Brielle."

What a pretty name!

"I'll take a Caramel Banana Blast," Shreya says through her wide smile, barely able to contain her anticipation at trying it.

"Comin' right up!" Brielle says, then turns to fill the cup at the dispenser.

Shreya watches the whole time as Brielle tops the concoction with sea salt caramel drizzle, banana frosted chunks and candied pecans. *Yum!*

"Oh, that looks so good!" Shreya squeals as Brielle passes

the cup to her, and she hands her credit card over as payment.

Brielle giggles as she swipes the card. "I haven't seen you around her before. Are you just passing through?"

"No, I just moved here," Shreya replies, thrilled at this new topic. "Do you by any chance go to Mirror Point High? I'm starting next week."

"Actually, I do," Brielle says with a warm smile.

"Awesome!" Shreya puts her hand across the counter and places it excitedly on Brielle's wrist. "I'm so happy I've made my first friend! I'm Shreya, by the way. I can't wait to see you at school!"

Brielle's smile widens and a charming blush brightens her cheeks as she hands the card back to Shreya. "Uh, yeah, me too."

Brimming with joy, Shreya plucks a spoon from the collection beside the buffet glass, scoops up a bite and puts it in her mouth. Her eyes roll up into her head as she savors the salty-sweet goodness.

"You're a genius," Shreya gushes, her mouth still half full. "This is exactly what I needed right now."

"Er, thanks," Brielle says, chuckling behind a wobbly, slightly embarrassed smile, and Shreya is also certain that she likes this girl very much.

Suddenly realizing she needs to thank the blond girl for the awesome suggestion as well as introduce herself, she spins around, calls "Later," to Brielle, and heads for the door.

Her smile falters when she realizes the group of teens are no longer sitting out here, and Shreya puffs her lower lip out in a disappointed pout.

Oh well, she knows she'll run into the blond girl again eventually. These things are always a matter of time for her.

"Yes, I've got it," says a smooth male voice to her left in a hushed tone. "I won't let you down."

She turns just in time to see an extremely hot guy with short black hair and russet eyes hang up on a phone call and stride past her. Her heart flutters when he flashes her a sexy grin as he passes. That boy is danger wrapped in chocolate with a cherry on top. She licks her lips as she watches him go inside, and not from the sugar left from her last bite.

The guy goes behind the counter and pecks Brielle on the cheek. Huh, she wouldn't have pegged the sweet girl Brielle as having a thing for bad boys. But then again, who doesn't?

Mr. Tall, Dark and Dangerous is officially off limits. I'm not about to mess with my new bestie!

Besides, it's not like she ever has any trouble finding a boy to play with. That guy Zach wasn't half bad looking.

She shrugs and goes to sit at a table in the center of the seating area, and pops another delicious spoonful into her mouth, practically moaning from the sinful flavors dancing around her tongue. When she recovers from her swoon and opens her eyes, a glint on the floor catches her eyes, and she turns her head down to look at it.

Laying on the cement floor beside her table is an ornate key made of pale metal. It's so pretty! She wonders what it could possibly go to, if anything at all. It looks far too decorative to actually be useful. Maybe it's just a jewelry piece.

At that thought, she decides to pick it up, determined to take it home and make a kickass necklace out of it. That should make an excellent first-day-of-school accessory!

When she bends over to reach for it, she sees a folded twenty dollar bill a few inches from it.

"This is so my lucky day!" she chirps as she reaches for the bill as well.

When she straightens back up, she catches the eye of yet another hottie striding past with sandy blond hair and to-die-for sky blue eyes. Eyes that are set firmly on her.

Flaring a flirtatious brow at him, she waves with a coy, "Hi there."

His only response is a narrowing of those sexy eyes and a curt chin jut before he goes into Creamy Dreams without another look in her direction.

Who knew this sleepy little town would be so full man candy?

I think I'm going to like it here!

TRISTAN

Tristan's not sure why he does this to himself. But as he enters Creamy Dreams, his gaze instantly finding Brielle, then a second later Kerrim—because the douche is never far away—he tortures himself anyway. It seems it's become his new hobby.

Brielle notices him and throws him a quick smile as she serves a customer, her dark hair up in a ponytail, making her look sweet and fresh. Kerrim smirks at him from behind the counter.

Tristan pulls up a strained smile and looks away. He really shouldn't be here. He hasn't enjoyed a fro-yo since Brielle and Kerrim became a thing. He hasn't enjoyed much of anything.

Which probably makes him just as much of a douche as Kerrim. He should be happy that Brielle's moved on. That she has someone in her life.

But I'm not, he admits to himself as he flops onto his usual seat. There's something about Kerrim that unsettles Tristan, and he's determined that it's not just the green-eyed monster that's taken residence amongst his ribs.

It's one of the reasons he keeps watching. He's waiting for the guy to slip up.

That, and he just can't stay away.

"Here you go. Your favorite," says Brielle, sliding a fro-yo loaded with gummy bears across the table.

Tristan looks up, bracing himself for the inevitable jolt when his gaze connects with hers. Yep, there it is. "Thanks."

Brielle looks away, and he's never sure what the pink tinge on her cheeks means. Probably that his intensity unnerves her... She goes back behind the counter where Kerrim slips a possessive arm around her shoulder and presses a kiss to her temple, his eyes on Tristan.

Tristan looks away, knowing he can't pretend to smile right now. Not when he wants to smash his fist in the guy's face. Instead, he scoops up a spoonful of the fro-yo, trying not to scowl at the gummy bear smiling up at him, and shoves it in his mouth. Brielle brought him this, and he's damned well going to pretend to enjoy it.

Taking some satisfaction in grinding up the gummy bear, he pulls out his cell phone and scrolls through his feed. In part, to distract himself. But also to check what's happening in the world. It's been a week since Aqua was destroyed and they learned its people were rescued by the Ark. And there's been nothing since then. Esther hasn't detected any changes in dark matter. No Skins. No new Zodiac Guardian.

No idea what to do next.

Tristan keeps scrolling, although he's not sure what for. It's not like reports of the Ark are going to pop up on his socials. Well, he freaking hopes not, anyway. Mentions of the Zodiacs have only just started declining.

And because they have to find the Ark before Chardis does.

Jamming his spoon in the melting fro-yo, and sinking a good three or four grinning gummy bears in the process,

Tristan finds himself back on the endless merry-go-round that his mind has been on. To find the Ark, they need the book that Zarius and Tessa had. Tristan's sure it'll give them some idea of how to find it. But Jack has the book.

And Jack isn't exactly on speaking terms with the Zodiacs.

Tristan pulls out his cell phone again, dialing Veronica's number. Maybe she or Logan have some news.

"Hey, Tristan," says Veronica. "I'm just on my way to meet Jareth, and no, I don't have any news."

He clamps his mouth shut. "Maybe I was calling to say hi."

She snorts. "Logan and I told you we'd call as soon as we know anything." She pauses. "We've also told you Dad is keeping his cards close to his chest."

"Yeah, I know," Tristan says heavily. Jack is well aware his two children have links to the Zodiacs. He's not sure whether he can trust them. That would be a sucky place to be for both Veronica and Logan.

"We're still getting the same response if we bring it up—he'll give you the book if you give him Dyad."

"Not. Happening," growls Tristan. Dyad may have done some shady things in the past, but Ada's a Zodiac now.

"I know, I know," Veronica says on a sigh. "It's not an option. But it means it'll take some time while we try to find a Plan B. We need a bargaining chip of some kind."

"Thanks. I'll keep thinking," says Tristan.

They hang up and he glares at his cell as if it's at fault. There's only so many dead ends a guy can reach before he feels like throwing it at something.

The door opens and Ada enters, making Tristan glance at his watch. Was she listening in? She scans the café and finds Tristan, then strides over and sits down, shoving her mass of red hair over her shoulder. "I've got news."

He glances at the phone on his wrist. "You didn't want to

call me?" Ada loves using all the amazing tech she's outfitted the Zodiacs with.

"I was going to," she says, glancing around once more in a way that has Tristan tensing. He finds himself doing the same, his gaze quickly skipping over Brielle and Kerrim as they laugh at something between themselves. "Until I saw that the change in dark matter was here, at Creamy Dreams."

Tristan's gaze flies back to Ada. "Here? Now?"

She nods. "Esther just picked it up."

Tristan's once again scanning the café, wondering if Esther detected friend or foe. Skin or Zodiac. But it's only the four of them inside—himself, Ada, Brielle and Kerrim.

The door opens again, the bell tinkling above, and the girl he saw outside skips in. She's short with pixie blond hair streaked with pink and a permanent smile. She approaches the counter and practically bounces like she's Tigger reincarnated. "Can I have another of those delicious caramel banana blasts, please."

Tristan's eyebrows shoot up. He saw her eating a large when he entered. She obviously doesn't count calories. Maybe Cassandra could spend some time with her. Then his eyebrows hike another inch as another thought strikes him.

He turns back to Ada. Surely not…

She shrugs, her eyes shrewd and assessing as she watches the girl. Have they found the next Zodiac?

Or is she a Skin…

Deciding they need to find out, Tristan ambles up to the counter. "You should definitely try the flaked chocolate pieces on top."

The girl looks up at him, her hazel eyes almost sparkling, they're so guileless. And no silver ring around the iris, so not a Skin. "Ooh, I love chocolate." She turns to Brielle. "Double helping of chocolate flakes, thanks."

"Sure thing," Brielle says, glancing in curiosity at Tristan.

He keeps his focus on the girl. "Hi, my name's Tristan. You must be new around here?"

"Yep, just moved here. I'm Shreya."

"Nice to meet you." He smiles as he leans a hip against the counter. "You must love your fro-yo to have a second one."

Shreya slaps a twenty-dollar bill down and slides it to Brielle. "Yep," beams the girl. "I found a nice little surprise tucked in the pocket of my jeans. Figured it was a sign I should have another fro-yo."

Brielle and Tristan glance at each other. He saw the girl pick up the money from the pavement just before he entered, and Brielle's subtle shake of her head confirms what he suspected. The girl's lying.

But why?

"Did you want to join me?" he asks, indicating the table he was sitting at. "I could get you up to speed on Mirror Point."

"Wow, the guys around here work fast," says Shreya, angling her head. She takes a step back, bringing her fro-yo with her.

Tristan holds his hands up. "I just want to chat," he says. "Promise." The last thing he wants to do is scare her off.

But Shreya's already taken another step back. "Well, if it's meant to be, we'll bump into each other soon." With an impish grin, she spins with the grace of a ballerina and skips out the door.

Tristan blinks as he wonders if the dark matter disturbance was something else. Surely Shreya can't be the next Zodiac Guardian.

She's just too…cheery.

JACK

15:37

Jack pops two antacids into his mouth and chews, grinding them to a paste. Washing it down with a gulp of cold coffee, he decides to take two more.

He's going to need them.

He glares at the book in front of him. He was excited in a way he hasn't been in a long time when he found it jammed into a wall cavity at a run-down motel. He knew it was significant if so many people were interested in it. It felt good to have one up on Tristan. Jack couldn't wait until he got to Nebula HQ so he could see what's inside.

Except, that was weeks ago, and the excitement has well and truly soured.

He flips it open, cursing as it does what it always does whenever he opens it. The words on the page disappear. As if they're allergic to daylight.

Jack's tried everything. Opening it in a dark room. UV light. X-ray. Infrared. Gamma rays. He even tried photographing the damned pages the moment the book opened.

But each time he's had the same outcome—all he gets is a blank page.

He slams it shut with a growl. He suspects he doesn't have the technology to unlock whatever information the book contains. Because it's not of this world.

Jack reaches for his bottle of antacids again. He's about to tip out a handful when his cell rings.

"Yes?" he barks. He's not in the mood for more bad news.

"Cadbury, we need to meet."

Jack's eyebrows jolt up. "Of course, Senator," he says, his tone far more moderate. "I'm free tomorrow night?"

"Excellent. I'll see you at the usual place."

The line goes dead, leaving Jack staring at the blank screen.

What does Senator Harrison Fitzgerald want with him now?

CASSANDRA

C assandra waits in the bushes outside her old house for several minutes, debating what her next move should be.

She's been following her father to try and figure out exactly what he's up to. Solomon told Brielle that they were working for Chardis before, but now their allegiances are changing as they try to pick the winning side. Cassandra doesn't trust anything they could tell them. Both he and her father are professional liars. If she wants the truth, she has to see for herself what her father does when he thinks no one's watching.

And naturally, it was just her luck that her father went home. The one place she doesn't want to go. She doesn't even think her key still works—no doubt they'd have changed the locks by now—but even if it did, she'd be a fool to follow her father inside.

Except she needs to see and hear everything he does behind closed doors. The book. The Ark. And Chardis lurking, waiting. There's too much at stake.

Finally deciding on a course of action, she creeps around

the back of the house, peering through the windows. The living room is empty, and she's fairly certain he's in his office. That's pretty much the only room he ever uses when he's not sleeping.

Scaling the exterior wall, she hugs up beside the office window and cranes her head just enough to peek inside.

There he is, just as she figured, sitting at his desk and talking—more like yelling—to someone on his cell phone.

Hunkering down, she kneels as close to the windowsill as she can. Luckily, the loud register of her dad's voice carries through the single paned glass.

"Do you have any idea how gravely you screwed up by not getting to it first?" he barks into the phone, and she hates how she flinches at the anger in his tone after all this time, after she's finally free of his wrath. "Now the damn FBI has the book. We needed that as leverage."

He pauses to let whoever's on the other end defend themself, and she wonders who that might be. Pitch only knows how many people he's got under his thumb.

"I don't want to hear it, Solomon!" he snaps.

Solomon? Didn't he get arrested by the FBI?

"I don't even know why I bothered to bail you out. You're useless."

Ah, that explains it. There's very little daddy's money can't buy. She sneers in disgust as she continues to listen.

"Don't call me again unless you have *something* of value to offer." He hangs up the call without giving Solomon a chance to respond and leans back in his leather swivel chair.

Cassandra adjusts her weight and her foot snaps a twig. She barely manages to duck out of sight before her father's head turns in her direction. She clasps her hands over her mouth, as if that will somehow make her invisible, hoping he won't feel inclined to open the window and investigate.

"Damn cats," he mutters, and relief forces out the breath she'd been holding.

"Where Solomon has failed, I assure you that I will not."

At this stranger's voice, Cassandra cranes her neck back up to look inside. There's a man standing in the corner of the office, dressed in a dark brown trench coat and a black bowler hat that casts a shadow over his face.

"I sure hope so," her dad grouses. "Good help is so hard to come by these days."

"We're getting very close to locating the Staff," the hatted man informs.

Staff?

"I'm certain we'll have it within the week."

"Excellent, excellent," her father says, braiding his fingers on his lap like a bond villain. All that's missing is a fluffy white cat for him to pet. "Let me know as soon as you have it."

"Of course, sir." The man nods, then takes his leave of the room.

Forget following her father. Cassandra needs to know who this guy is and, more importantly, what the heck this staff thingy is.

She slinks around the house and hugs her back to the corner as the man heads out the front door to a black sedan parked across the street and down a few houses. If that isn't shady as hell, she doesn't know what is.

As soon as he gets in, she goes to head for the Uber she paid double to wait for her around the bend when, suddenly, a hand clamps something over her mouth from behind. The scent that fills her nostrils is strong and chemical, and she can't help but inhale it as she lets out a scream of retaliation.

And everything goes black.

VERONICA

The house is strangely quiet when Veronica walks
through the front door.

"Jareth?" she calls out, waiting as only the ticking grand-
father clock responds to her.

Jareth asked her to meet him here when she got out of
school—she really envies that Mirror Point High had two
weeks of Fall Break instead of just one like her school. But
according to the complete silence ringing through the house,
he's not here. Where could he have gone off to? Isn't it a guy's
job to stay in his underwear and play video games all day
when school's out?

The idea of Jareth in nothing but his boxers floods heat
up her neck, and her desire to see him becomes a full-on
need.

Maybe he's down in HQ? Even as she thinks it, she finds it
unlikely, as Esther would've notified anyone in HQ of a visi-
tor, but Veronica literally can't not check.

"Good afternoon, Veronica," Esther's maternal voice
greets her as she enters the room full of computer screens
and gadgets that she wished she understood.

"Uh yeah," Veronica replies, feeling strange talking to a disembodied voice. She likes making eye contact when she talks to someone. But then again, Esther isn't really a *someone*... Is she?

Veronica shakes that confusion away and gets to the point. "Have you seen Jareth?" *That's a stupid question. Of course, she hasn't seen Jareth, she doesn't have eyes!* "I mean, has he been in here recently?"

"Jareth was last in this room exactly seventeen minutes and twenty-one seconds ago," Esther says.

Veronica can't help but frown at the overly precise answer. "Do you have any idea where he went?"

"I don't have ideas," Esther replies robotically.

Veronica grits her teeth in frustration at her own vernacular that's apparently confusing the computer chick. "Er, I mean, do you know where he went?"

A moment's pause.

"According to the GPS tracker on his wristwatch, he is at Stop and Go," Esther informs.

Veronica twists her lips in curiosity. "I wonder what he's doing there."

"He appears to be eating a hotdog," Esther says, answering the question Veronica hadn't actually meant to ask.

Veronica's brows press tight together, and she shakes her head in consternation. "Wait, how do you know he's eating a hotdog?"

No words come from the speakers around the room, but the largest of the screens directly across from Veronica fills with an unfortunately angled view of the underside of Jareth's chin and neck as he shoves a ketchup and mustard dripping hotdog into his mouth, the bright fluorescent ceiling lights shining on either side of his head.

"What the...?" Veronica stammers as she stares open-mouthed at the screen. "How am I seeing him?"

"There's a camera on the face of all the Zodiac Guardians' watches," Esther explains.

"Whoa!" Veronica breathes. *Apparently, Esther does have eyes.*

With a sudden jolt of mild horror, Veronica remembers how many times she and Jareth have been intimate while he's wearing the watch. Esther has seen parts of her she probably hasn't even seen, and from the worst possible angles, too! Heat blazes in her cheeks, and she makes a mental note to make Jareth take the watch off from now on.

"Maybe I'll just wait for him in the living room," Veronica says, pointing at the door.

Esther says nothing, and Veronica shakes her head, wondering why the heck she was waiting for a response before she heads out into the hallway.

Her feet, having a mind of their own, lead her into the kitchen, and she raids the fridge in hopes of a can of cola. No sooner does she open the fridge door than her phone buzzes in her bra—the sweater leggings she chose to wear today might be warm and cute, but they don't have any pockets, which is seriously annoying.

With a small level of difficulty, she fishes the device from between her cleavage and looks at the screen. There's no phone number, only the word "Restricted" as the phone continues to vibrate in her hand. Narrowing her eyes slightly, she swipes the little green phone button and presses the phone to her ear. "Hello?"

"The Zodiacs are in danger," says a smooth female voice, and panic bolts through Veronica's body like Ada just zapped her.

Swallowing with a suddenly dry throat, Veronica asks, "Who is this?"

"Meet me at Middleton Park on Cherry Avenue in fifteen

minutes, and I'll explain everything," the mysterious caller says. "Come alone," then the line goes dead.

Veronica stares at the blanking screening for several long seconds, her heart feeling like it's going to slam itself out of her chest like the creature from *Alien*.

Should she go? What if this is a trap?

Whoever that was obviously knows Veronica is tied in with the Zodiacs, and Veronica realizes that, for the sake of her friends and boyfriend, she has to meet this person.

Decisively shoving her phone back between her boobs and closing the fridge, she heads out the door to find out what exactly this person knows and what they plan to do with that knowledge.

5

BRIELLE

As Brielle steps onto the still-moist grass, she questions her logic as to why she came to meet this shady character a second time. Yet, one mysterious phone call is all it took. Even though the last time, the FBI had shown up, and she narrowly escaped getting taken in for questioning herself. Not to mention how exactly had Solomon managed to get out of FBI custody, anyway? Or had he?

What if she's about to meet with an escaped felon? What if the FBI rock up again and take her this time for good?

What if she winds up in a cell right alongside her adopted father, Frank? Poor Bea would be all alone then.

Brielle can't bear the thought of that, but some small part of her knows that she needs to hear whatever Solomon has to say. Solomon is—or was—in with Chardis. From the sounds of things the last they'd spoken, that was no longer the case. If Solomon was now on Chardis's crap list, he must need the aid of the Zodiacs, and that could only be beneficial for them.

Because Solomon knows things they don't. Knows more about Chardis than they do.

She has to do this.

With that thought in mind, she proceeds across the lawn to the bench under the oak tree his message had specified.

This time of year, Central Park is brimming with people who are trying to cram as much nature and sunshine into the last warm-ish days before the frost sets in. She's grateful for that. It means fewer chances of getting ambushed by Skins, or the second worst threat—FBI agents. With this many witnesses, she'll have safety from attack. Also, with this many people going about their own business, jogging with their headphones on, she'll also get a certain amount of privacy.

Best of both worlds.

Anxiety sizzling down her spine, and goosebumps rising on her flesh that isn't due to the chill in the air, Brielle sits on the bench.

And waits.

It's too bad she's here under such precarious circumstances. The sun is warm as it shines down on her through the branches of the tree above, and ducks are even wading in the pond several yards in front of her, with happy park-goers tossing them bits of bread.

She laughs as an outraged goose honks when an overly brave mother gets too close, then runs back to the stroller she'd momentarily abandoned to try and feed it.

Everyone at this park seems so happy, so carefree. She can't help but wonder what that would be like. To go about her life without a care in the world. Even before she knew she was a Zodiac, she'd never had that life. There'd always been another shoe about to drop.

She just never expected a shoe of this magnitude to fall into her lap and attempt to crush her for the rest of time.

Suddenly, a large body plops onto the bench beside her, breaking her soliloquy and forcing her back to the present.

"Don't turn to me," he says immediately. "It will raise suspicion."

She stops herself mid-turn and faces back forward, noticing out of the corner of her eye that her new neighbor —Solomon, by the sound of his voice—is wearing an innocuous hoodie, a far cry from his usual suit.

"Pretend to be scrolling on your phone as we talk, and I'll do the same," he instructs in a confidential tone.

She does as he says, pulling out her phone and swiping the screen on.

"Why did you ask me to meet you?" she asks, staring down at the idle screen.

"The FBI has the book," he says.

She doesn't need to ask what book he's referring to. Tristan told all of them about that episode.

"Yes," is all she says.

"We need to get it from them."

"Why?" She almost turns to him when he hisses at her to stop, and she glares back down at her phone again.

"It contains valuable information that could help Chardis win this war," he replies. "We can't let that happen."

She shakes her head. "I don't understand why you care. You were once on his side. Why the sudden mutiny?"

He's silent for a moment, and she heightens her lie sensitivity for whatever he's about to say.

"When we realized what his ultimate plans were, we knew we could no longer ally ourselves with him."

No alarms. "'We' meaning you and Richard Sinclair?" she asks.

"Yes," he says after a brief pause, letting her know there are more people involved than just the two of them.

"And what is Chardis planning?" she asks, lowering her voice even more when she says his name.

Another pause, and his voice is deeper when he speaks. "Destruction. Complete and utter destruction."

Brielle's heart thuds against her lungs at that, making breathing more of a struggle for a second.

"We need to get that book before Chardis does," he continues.

Realizing she must look silly staring blankly down at her phone, she opens Snapchat and begins blindly scrolling through her feed. "Again, does 'we' mean you and Mr. Sinclair, or 'us'?"

"As of right now, that designation isn't important, only that the book is made secure from Chardis," he answers, and she's about to quip a remark at him when he says, "The safest place for it would be in the hands of the Zodiacs."

She closes her lips and thinks on that for a moment.

"And there's something else," he preludes.

She holds her breath as she waits for him to continue.

"Have you ever heard of the Staff?"

She blinks hard several times, not sure what context his question is even in.

"Er, no?" her reply comes out as a question at the end.

"There is an artifact known as the Staff. We must also find it before Chardis does. It could be the key to destroying him forever. The book holds the location of the Staff."

Brielle's heart beats an excited tune, and she wonders why she's never heard of such an item before. Does Tristan know about it? Could such a thing really even exist?

"Why are you coming to me about all of this?" she can't help but ask. Her, the weakest of all the Zodiacs. Is that why? Is she the limping gazelle, an easy target to prey upon, a lamb ripe for the slaughter? "Why not go directly to Tristan? He's the one in charge, the one with the most sway."

She can see Solomon shake his head in her peripheral vision, and a chuckle rumbles deeply through him. "Firstly, the Staff will inflict great harm on the Geminis if they touch it. And second, you really have no idea how powerful you are, do you?"

Her eyes widen as she stares blankly down at one of her classmates' posts on her phone. What?

"I came to you because, for one, I know you'll trust me when I come to you candidly," he begins. "I know you can sense when someone lies, and unlike the others—Tristan especially—you'll know that what I say is valid. But it's more than that. I sense a great power in you, perhaps one you're not even aware of yet. I suspect that you'll be the key to ending this war once and for all. That is why I've always called on you. It was just luck, or fate, of whatever you want to call it, that it was you who came into Richard's employ when you did. If it had been any of the others, this situation wouldn't have worked. But you... Never doubt that you have a greater sway in this war than anyone else, even Tristan." He speaks Tristan's name like it leaves a sour taste in his mouth, and this whole conversation really sends her reeling.

What power could he possibly see in her that she hadn't stumbled upon yet? Sure, she could hurt Chardis with her penance power, but that did nothing to the Skins, which are basically his entire army. And she's seen for herself that, even hitting Chardis with the other Zodiacs' powers at the same time, she couldn't defeat him. How could Solomon think she could play any vital part in this Universal battle?

"Do whatever you can to reprieve Jack Cadbury of that book. I'll be in touch if I hear anything more about the Staff." And then Solomon rises and walks away, leaving her to stare at the black screen of her sleeping phone as she processes everything he just said.

Suddenly, her screen lights up, a text from Kerrim appearing in a bubble at the top.

We need to talk. Where are you? I'll pick you up.

Brielle is too shaken by the recent conversation to worry too much about what this text means, so she quickly replies that she's at Central Park. Whatever it is, at least she'll have a ride home.

Okay. Be there in ten.

By the time she crosses the park and reaches the entrance, Kerrim's sleek black Mustang is already waiting on the curb, its engine still running.

She mildly wonders if he's about to tell her he's making another sudden trip again as she opens the passenger door and gets inside. Kerrim's handsome face, which is usually fixed in a devil-may-care expression, is set with a serious one.

"What's up?" she asks tenuously, sudden concern for him tightening her chest. Did something happen to his dad? He never really talks about his family, and it dawns on her how little she really knows about Kerrim. Not that she's ever pushed to ask.

His brows pinch together, and he seems to be debating his words. "I've been keeping this secret for long enough, but I can't stand quietly by anymore."

Before she can ask what he means by that, he holds up his left hand, and from thin air, tangible shadows appear and weave through his fingertips.

"Brielle, I know you're a Zodiac," he says, his sexy voice dark and gravelly. "Because I am, too."

JACK

22:43

Senator Fitzgerald is already waiting for Jack at the street corner they'd agreed on. The lighting is poor in this section of the city, which is deliberate. Jack doubts this meeting was entered into the Senator's schedule. It's strictly off the books.

Jack stops beside him, leaning against the wall in the same way the Senator is. No one can creep up from behind this way. And they have a clear line of sight of the street around them. A drunk woman stumbles further down the block, riffling in her purse. After long seconds she pulls out a set of keys, needs three attempts to get them into the door she's beside, then disappears into the dinghy building.

It's once they're alone that the Senator speaks. "What do you know of the Zodiacs?"

Jack stills. That wasn't a question he was expecting. He did some digging around about Senator Harrison Fitzgerald. Ex-army and an Ivy League graduate, what's most surprising about him is that he's African American. This man worked harder than most to get where he is.

Jack jams his hands in his pockets, conscious things have now gotten political. "I'm not in a position to comment on that."

"You are now," says the Senator, keeping his voice low. "I've been appointed by the United States government to oversee Nebula. We're very interested now that it's public knowledge the Zodiac superheroes exist."

Years of training keep Jack's face neutral as he digests the surprising news. No one told him someone was being appointed higher up. And exactly how high does this go?

What's more, can he trust Senator Fitzgerald? Jack didn't get where he is assuming the answer is yes.

"I don't know as much as I'd like," he says grudgingly.

"They're flying around in suits, not answering to anyone as far as we know," says the Senator. "And no one knows their identity. That's a very definite threat to the United States."

"We know they're extra-terrestrial. And their technology

is advanced. We have some leads, but nothing concrete yet." Jack omits that at least one of those leads is his daughter. He's keeping Veronica out of this until he understands exactly what's going on.

"We need to catch them," growls the Senator. "You'll have access to whatever resources you need."

Jack nods. Nebula was already quite well resourced, but now he's been given a blank check. His mind is already whirling as he considers the possibilities.

A door opens to their left, and a cat is thrown onto the street, hissing and spitting. The door slams shut again, but it's enough to remind them that it's time for this meeting to come to a close.

Senator Fitzgerald pushes away from the wall, tugging the collar of his jacket up a little higher. "Find them. Catch them. And bring them to me in Washington," he orders. He strides away, not expecting an answer.

Obviously expecting results.

Jack walks away in the opposite direction, his stride long and determined.

It's only a matter of time before Tristan and his friends have a little visit to D.C.

6

CASSANDRA

Voices slowly carry into Cassandra's rousing consciousness. Her head is pounding like she's being repeatedly kicked by a racehorse, and her stomach churns with a mild nausea. She wants to open her eyes, but her lids feel too heavy to lift.

The voices grow clearer, cutting through the fog in which she's floating, and she recognizes them as those of her dad and…someone else…

The man in the hat…

That's right! She was about to follow him when—

With that realization, she forces her eyes open. All she can do is squint, but her other senses return to her as her surroundings come blurrily into view.

She's in what appears to be some sort of basement, and her dad—or should she just refer to him as Richard now seeing as he's no longer and never really was a father to her —and Creepy Hat Guy are standing in front of her.

Only…Richard isn't quite himself. A pair of horrendous, curved black horns are protruding from the top of his salt and pepper hair. His suit blazer is blood red, and where a pair of slacks should be below that is a pair of furry black hooves and a forked tail that whips this way and that like that of a bored cat.

I must be dreaming, she thinks groggily.

"…fortuitous that we found her following you," Richard is saying. "She may be the ransom we need to ensure the book comes our way."

"Solomon says he has a plan to get the book on his own, but he's failed us so many times, I'm unconvinced he'll come through on that," Creepy Hat Guy says. "She makes a good Plan B, just as long the Zodiacs don't go to the FBI with this."

Or maybe I'm not dreaming. But what the hell is going on?

Suddenly, thousands of hand-sized black spiders with tall, spindly legs emerge from the walls as if rising from pools of ink and scramble toward Cassandra like she's the biggest fly they've ever seen.

Panic saturates her entire being like hot molten lead and she lets out a squeak of fright as she struggles to flee.

But she can't move!

She looks down, and her horror impossibly hikes to a near heart-exploding level as she sees that she's trapped in a massive web, fully encased from the chest down in sticky white cottony threads. The spiders are going to eat her!

She squeezes her eyes shut as she struggles with all her strength, but even if her body wasn't as limp as a wet noodle, the web-ball around her doesn't budge.

"Ah, look who's finally awake," Richard purrs darkly.

When she opens her eyes again, confusion makes her head throb. The spiders are gone as if they'd never been there. She looks down at her body, and the web is no longer there, either. Instead, she's tied to an uncomfortable wooden chair, bound around her chest and upper arms, wrists and ankles with what feels like thick rope.

"What the hell?" she gasps, shaking her head in hopes of clearing it.

"Nasty drug, fentanyl," Richard says as he stalks toward her, his devil's tail flicking from side to side. "While it's excellent for its sedative and inhibitive properties, it can cause horrible hallucinations." He bends down to look her in the eye. "I wonder what nightmares you're seeing right now." His lips curl into a wicked grin, and his eyes blaze red like powerful infernos as they pierce into her.

Swallowing her terror, Cassandra summons her hatred for this man to speak. "You *drugged* me?"

Richard straightens and shrugs, ringing the inside of his left cuff with his right index finger. "We had to be sure you wouldn't use your powers against us."

Testing his words, she calls heat to her palms, ready to show him exactly what she's made of. But the weakness that's invaded every one of her extremities seems to have also doused her fire.

"Shit," she curses.

A dark chuckle rumbles out of Richard's throat like a roll of thunder before a storm, seeming to echo in the small space.

"Now, why don't you tell us why you were following us?" he demands.

She glares at him defiantly, but the words tumble out of her like rocks falling down a steep hill. "I don't trust you, and I needed to see what you were up to." She bites down hard on her lip as if to punish it for betraying her.

He laughs again, apparently pleased with her frustration.

Her eyes dart to Creepy Hat Guy, and she has to blink several times. Under that brown hat where a face should be, there are hundreds of roaches and centipedes crawling over each other in a repulsive ball, and the nausea that had only been slight before now feels all-consuming.

"You're such an utter disappointment," Richard says, and she's relieved for a reason to look away. "You failed to be a worthy daughter, and you can't even sneak up on me successfully."

His words sting, tearing at old wounds inside her soul.

Don't let him beat you down.

"If anyone's a failure here, it's you as a father," she sneers with all the hatred she feels for him. "All you had to do was love me, but you're not capable of feeling anything for anyone."

His red eyes narrow at her, flames licking over his eyelids. "It's not my fault there's nothing worth loving about you."

Hatred and rage boil in her chest, and she wishes that same fire would burn in her palms. She'd love nothing more than to set him ablaze right here and now. "Well, I guess the apple doesn't fall far from the tree, then, does it?"

Faster than she can even brace herself, the back of his hand crashes into Cassandra's cheek, and her world spins as her head careens to the side.

"You'll speak when asked," he snaps. "Or haven't I taught you that already?"

Agony spreads over the left side of her skull, and her vision struggles to right itself as she props her head back up.

He'd never hit her like that before. All the years she lived with him as his daughter, he'd never hit her anywhere that could be visible to others. It was always the belt to the back. Looks like those old rules don't apply anymore.

"Where is the Staff?" he demands.

Her head rolls loosely from side to side as she shakes it. "I have no idea what you're talking about." It even hurts to speak.

"Hmm, that's too bad," he says, rubbing his chin.

She glares up at him from her head's downcast position.

"The others will come for me. They'll do everything they can to rescue me."

He bends down at eye level with her again and grins wickedly. "Oh, I'm counting on it."

7

VERONICA

A chill races over Veronica's arms as she makes her way onto the lawn of Middleton Park, raising goosebumps that almost prickle against the fabric of her leather jacket. Her muscles are tight all over, ready to sprint to safety if this proves to be a trap.

But when she spots the only figure in the entire space sitting at a picnic table, her apprehension wanes. The figure is very clearly a woman, wearing a mauve sweater and her hair up in a loose bun. Veronica isn't sure what she expected to see when she got here, but this unassuming, casually dressed woman isn't it.

Veronica sweeps her eyes over the small square of Middleton Park a second time, but no one else is here. This park, perhaps the size of three property blocks blended together and housing a jungle gym on one side, sits in the middle of a cul-de-sac and is usually frequented by mothers with their toddlers. But there are no children frolicking about, and not a stroller in sight.

This woman must be who she's here to meet.

Feigning indifference, Veronica stuffs her hands in her

pockets and plops down on the other side of the picnic table, facing away from the woman and watching her breath materialize in the air as it leaves her mouth.

Neither of them says anything, and Veronica begins to wonder if she'd gotten this all wrong. Maybe this woman wasn't here for her, and she's invading her personal space for no reason.

Veronica sighs and begins to rise from the seat.

"Thank you for meeting me," the woman says behind her.

So, she wasn't wrong.

Veronica whirls around, hopping her legs over the bench seat to face her mysterious caller.

The woman's face is smooth and oddly sweet, and, like the rest of her, so ordinary that Veronica's certain she could blend in just about anywhere. She's not wearing makeup, her hair appears to have been lazily twirled into that bun, and her clothes are so simple, there's no way anyone would need to take a second look at her.

Maybe that's intentional…

"What do you want?" Veronica asks, deciding to cut to the chase.

A smirk tugs at the corners of the woman's lips, and she folds her arms over her chest. "Mostly, I want to warn you. Your father's organization isn't the only government sanctioned project established to oversee extra-terrestrial activity. Nebula was formed as a purely research-based project, but since the arrival of the Zodiacs, the U.S. military decided they needed an offensive force to combat them. They've formed a task force called Project Sunsign, with the sole purpose of tracking down and capturing the Zodiac Guardians."

Veronica's mouth dries up as it hangs open, lost for words for a moment. She puts up both hands. "Hang on. How do you know all of this? And who the heck are you?"

The woman nods. "My name is Vivian Styles," she offers, and Veronica rolls her eyes at her own fake name being used against her. "And I work for an anonymous organization called Operation Castle. We're not affiliated with any world governments and understand that the Zodiacs are not the true enemy our planet is facing."

Veronica doesn't fight the scowl that sets into her brow. "Okay, that answers the second question. You skipped over the first. How do you know so much about me?"

The so-called Vivian leans back, appraising Veronica with an appreciative gaze behind slightly narrowed fox-eyes. "We've been watching you, all of you. Any person of interest. We're quite sure we know of all the current Zodiacs' identities, as well as every single contact in all of their lives."

Veronica's scowl deepens, and she crosses her own arms in defiance. "Okay, so why don't you reach out to one of them? It's not like I'm their mascot or anything." Although, that would be pretty cool.

"We wanted to gain the trust of someone *they* trust first. We hope they can propose an alliance on our behalf," Vivian explains.

"And why would I do that?" Veronica quips. "You don't even have the decency to tell me your real name. Why would I ever trust you?"

Vivian's smirk grows to an all-out grin. "As someone who rarely plays with all the cards on the table, I'm sure you can appreciate why we are hiding our hand, as well. Once we've made certain that we've earned your trust, you will know exactly who and what we are."

Veronica's teeth clench, getting tired of the evasive bull this woman is giving her. "Again, why would I trust you if you're not willing to give me anything on faith?"

One of Vivian's finely plucked eyebrows arches upward in an almost-dare. "How about a tour of our facilities, and a detailed explanation of just how great of an ally we can be to your friends? But you have to come now, and alone."

Veronica's pulse quickens at that offer. If there really is an organization willing to help the Zodiacs, willing to thwart the advances of those who would threaten them, didn't she owe it to them to investigate?

Yet, this woman hasn't even given Veronica her real name. Trusting her would be downright stupid.

Veronica pushes to her feet, keeping her gaze on 'Vivian.' "No, thanks." She steps back. "When you're ready to be honest, call me."

Vivian's lips thin. "You mention this to the Zodiacs, and you'll never hear from me again."

Veronica spins around, her heart thudding even harder. She's taken a risk—she's banking that Vivian wants to talk to her again—but this feels right.

She's not outing Jareth and his friends unless she knows this woman's telling the truth.

At the same time, she knows she won't mention this to the Zodiacs.

Not when it could be the alliance they need.

8

SHREYA

Though the day has been wonderful, and Shreya's made plenty of new friends, she's feeling like a nap and would like to go home. A Google search on her phone told her that bus sixteen would take her closest to her new home, and as she arrives at the bus stop and makes herself comfortable on the bench, she wonders how long she'll have to wait for it.

Google also informed her that this bus arrives every hour on the hour, and seeing as the clock on the upper right hand corner of her phone screen reads five-o-four, she might've already missed it. Her sigh turns into a yawn as she realizes with melodrama that she really doesn't want to sit here for another hour.

Before she can even close her mouth on the dying yawn, she hears the huff of the bus as it stops on the curb in front of her.

Yay! Luck never seems to fail me!

The doors slide open with a lazy sort of groan, and she jumps to her feet and skips up the steps, sliding a dollar bill into the feeder before finding the first empty seat she can.

She looks at the faces of the few scattered passengers around her, and wonders which, if any of them, go to her new school.

She's never really had a chance to "lay roots" anywhere. Moving around every few months is the only life she's ever known, and rather than being sad each time she has to leave new friends behind, she just views each move as the next big adventure. Because of her parents' business, she's gotten to see so much of the country, and gotten to meet so many interesting people.

Being so close to New York, she can't wait to see what sort of fascinating characters are waiting for her to discover them. And who knows, one of the people on this very bus might just be her new best friend!

Just as the prospect sends butterflies aflutter in her belly, a girl who'd been looking at her gets up from her seat a few rows down and approaches to take the empty seat beside Shreya. The girl is about her age, with long black hair and a welcomingly pretty face. And her eyes—they're the strangest thing Shreya's ever seen! Soft hazel, a color that should be bright, but rimmed by a silver circle. How very interesting.

"You must be new in town," the girl says, offering a friendly smile.

Shreya notices that the smile doesn't reach her eyes, but she doesn't care, someone is being nice to her! "Yes, I am. I'm Shreya." She lifts her hand in a short wave.

"Nicky," the girl supplies in response. "I'd love to show you around all the best kept secrets." She winks, and something in her gaze makes Shreya's heart skip in a way she's not sure means danger or thrill—but either way, she's game to find out. Intrigue is what she lives for!

"That'd be great!" Shreya says. "I'm expected home soon, but I'd love to hang out tomorrow."

"Are you sure? There's a really neat spot at the next stop

—the place where all the cool kids hang out." Nicky lowers her thick dark lashes in another wink, and Shreya realizes that the next stop is where she gets off anyway. What's the harm?

"Okay, sure!"

The bus comes to halt, and Shreya follows Nicky down the steps and onto the sidewalk. She can see the impressive entrance of the Curacao Resort—the newest in her parents' chain of resorts—beckoning her across the street, but she knows they aren't expecting her for dinner for another hour, and even so, they've always been very lenient with her, so if she's a little late, as long as she lets them know where she is, she's sure they won't mind.

"It's just this way." Nicky nods in the opposite direction for Shreya to follow, and she has to almost jog to keep up with her. Nicky leads them into an alleyway, and the lights above the street they just left flicker on as dusk descends on this sleepy town.

"Where are we going?" Shreya asks, her pulse quickening with anticipation. She can't imagine what sort of "cool hang" could be at the other end of this alley. A secret night club perhaps? For this town, she'd be very surprised.

"We're almost there," Nicky replies without looking back.

For the first time, a whisper of something Shreya's never experienced tugs at her gut. Something…unpleasant, akin to the fear she's felt during horror films. Is it…suspicion?

In front of her, Nicky stops and puts her middle finger and thumb in her mouth, releasing a high-pitched whistle. Suddenly, two large men emerge from the thickening shadows on either side of her, like ghosts materializing, and grab both her arms.

"W-what's going on?" Shreya stutters, confused and wishing more than anything that she'd just gone home.

Nicky lets out a deep, menacing giggle and turns a wicked

grin on her. "You were so much easier to catch than I thought you'd be.

Her previously friendly tone is now mocking and snide. "I'm not so sure you really are the next Zodiac."

Zodiac? What's she talking about? What are they planning to do with her?

Someone, please help!

Just as suddenly as the two men appeared, they're wrenched from Shreya's sides. One of them is seizing on the floor, sparking with tendrils of electricity that crack off of him as he convulses, and the other is curled into a ball on the ground, grimacing like he's in the worst pain of his life.

Nicky shrieks and bolts down the alley faster than the same mysterious fate can befall her. What the—?

"Shreya?"

Shreya spins around to see a girl with wild orange curls and a blond guy standing behind her. Arcs of electricity dance over the girl's fingertips, and the guy seems to be concentrating as he glowers at the men on the ground.

"W-who are you?" Shreya asks, real fear coiling in her belly, and she doesn't like it one bit. "What's happening?"

"I'm not good with introductions, so I'm just going to be blunt," the girl begins. "We're Zodiac Guardians, and we believe you're one of us, otherwise these A-holes wouldn't have attacked you. But the only way to know for sure is if you come with us."

Zodiac Guardian, that's what Nicky must have meant. They think she's one of those superheroes? Ha! There's not a single thing about her that could be considered super, except for the awesome parents who adopted her and the unending supply of love they've always shown her.

And yet, Shreya feels no suspicion at all when she looks at these two strangers. It's not even intrigue or curiosity that draws her to them. It's a sense of almost nostalgia, that she knows them somehow. And she's certain that going with them is what she's supposed to do.

She takes one more look down at her attackers still writhing in pain on the ground. If she has some hidden power to do that, she needs to know what it is.

She looks up at her saviors. "Okay. Let's go."

BEATRICE

Bea traces the faint dent in the top of the dining room table, smiling faintly. The oval, mahogany expanse is one of the first things she and Frank bought after they were married. They planned on holding many a dinner at it, family, friends, investors.

It meant the day Frank dropped his knife on it after tasting her slow-cooked brisket, his eyes closed in pleasure, he suggested they replace it. But Bea refused. She presses the pad of her finger into the depression. It marked the moment Frank's face softened and melted as he appreciated the efforts she took to cook for him.

She never wanted to forget that moment.

Bea glances at her phone, the weight on her chest only multiplying. The house has been so quiet since Frank was arrested. Especially now that Brielle is...busy. There's been no reason to cook. It's probably a good thing. Bea's too worried most of the time to eat.

The cell rings and she snatches it. "Hello?"

"Mrs. Beatrice Pierce?"

"Yes, that's me."

"Are you willing to accept this call from Frank Pierce at the Mirror Point Penitentiary?"

"Yes, of course."

There's silence, then a *click*. Bea waits, her entire body frozen.

"Bea."

"Sweet lord, it's good to hear your voice," she breathes.

"Yours, too," says Frank, his voice tight. "How's Brielle?"

Bea smiles, the weight on her chest easing a little. They've barely said a word and she's already feeling better. "She misses you, just like I do." They'd just become a family and it was cruelly snatched away from them. She pulls in a breath. "I have good news and bad news."

"I'm all up for some good news right about now." She can just imagine the almost-smile on his dear face.

"The lawyers have found some discrepancies in the IRS audit of your companies. I'm not sure why it took so long to be found, but it's good news, nonetheless." She grips her cell phone a little tighter. "You could be out soon."

Frank lets out a long breath. "That is good news." He pauses. "I worry about you two."

She knows he does. It would be torture for him to be stuck in jail while the two women in his life deal with everything they're facing right now. Brielle is the daughter they always dreamed of.

"And the bad news?" he asks.

Bea chews her lip, hearing the way he's bracing himself. "I went to the hotel where the book was hidden, but it had already been taken."

There's another pause. Bea suspects her husband is cursing under his breath. "We can't afford for it to fall into the wrong hands. We need to find it, Bea."

"I know. I'm doing everything I can."

Frank sighs. "Of course, you are. Sorry, I have no doubt that's exactly what you're doing." There's another pause. "You know as well as I do what could happen if the wrong person finds the Staff."

A shudder ripples down Bea's spine. The prospect is one she won't let herself imagine.

There's a strident beep and a disembodied voice speaks. "One minute left."

Bea grits her teeth. The phone calls are never long enough. Neither are the visits. "Next update I'll give you in person. At home."

Frank chuckles and the sound is like a balm to her aching heart. "I'm looking forward to it. I love you, Bea."

"I love you, too, Frank."

They hang up before the penitentiary can do it for them, some small measure of control in an out-of-control situation.

Bea's hand drops heavily to her lap, still holding the phone. The weight is back, heavier and far more suffocating than before. *Please let him be out soon.*

The cell rings again and Bea frowns when she sees it's an unknown number. She picks up, already tense. "Hello?"

"It's me," says a female voice Bea instantly recognizes. "We need to meet. The Zodiacs are in danger."

9

BRIELLE

"How—what—who?" Brielle has so many questions, she doesn't know where to begin! She's just so utterly shocked that she can't seem to form any cohesive sentences in her frazzled mind.

All this time, Kerrim had been a Zodiac Guardian, and had known who and what she is. Should she be offended that he didn't tell her? Should she be even more offended that she's been dating him under false pretenses?

She silences those feelings, deciding to at least reserve judgment—and any resulting resentment—until she's heard the whole story.

He flattens his hand to stop her, and the snakelike shadows that were twisting around his fingers dissipate. "I'll explain everything, but I'd rather tell the story only once—to all the Zodiacs at the same time."

Her jaw clenches in impatient irritation, but she understands. "Fair enough," she grinds out. "Let's get to Tristan's house." At the mention of Tristan, her heart skips. How's he going to take this news? He already doesn't like Kerrim. There's no way he'll trust him after this deceit.

Honestly, Brielle's on the fence about that as well.

Kerrim nods and peels off the curb, racing through the typically maddening traffic of New York City with surprising stealth and precision.

She opens her phone screen and types out a text to Tristan. *Gather everyone. I've found another Zodiac.*

His reply is immediate. *Wow, I was just about to text you. We did, too! Everyone is already on their way.*

They found another Zodiac, as well? This day is getting way too weird, and it's almost more than she can handle.

Brielle can feel Kerrim's eyes on her as he drives, but she can't bring herself to meet them. She feels…betrayed. Why didn't he come out with this as soon as he met them? Why did he charm his way into her life—and heart—before telling her the truth? Was he using her? Has this whole fling between them been a farce?

"Look…I hope you don't hate me," he says, breaking the very tense silence. "I didn't mean to… I didn't know for sure…"

She turns to look at him finally, trying to keep her eyes from scowling. "Was any of this real? This…whatever it is, between you and me? Or were you just using me to get information?" Okay, forget reserving judgment, that ship has so sailed.

He frowns thoughtfully. "It wasn't exactly like that. I didn't know for sure you were a Zodiac when we met. I came here searching for the Zodiacs, and while I did sense something about you, I was also drawn to you personally. I didn't expect for us to get so…intimate, or for you to actually turn out to be who I was looking for. I know that doesn't help, but it's the way it happened. I just hope you don't hate me."

He gives her a hopeful, expectant look, and dammit if it doesn't make him look so alluring.

She looks out the window. "I haven't decided yet."

"Okay," he says, then returns his focus to the road.

They spend the rest of the drive to Tristan's in that same tenuous silence, and it's all Brielle can do not to voice every question that pops into her mind. So instead she logs them in her mental list to ask when they get with everyone.

They arrive at HQ, and she hurries inside ahead of him, wanting a little distance and knowing he'll follow. Inside the house, the living room is empty. Everyone must already be in the computer room.

With the new Zodiac.

Knowing Brielle's luck, they'll be the missing Gemini. The window that had opened with Kerrim's arrival in her life was closing, and now maybe the Tristan door will slam shut forever. The Universe must really hate her.

With heavy steps, she leads Kerrim to the command center. Inside, everyone but Cassandra and Veronica are here. Tristan is beaming as he looks at the new recruit and—

Holy pitch, it's the overly chipper girl from Creamy Dreams yesterday! Shreya!

Tristan turns his bright, eager expression on Brielle, but when Kerrim follows her into the room, his smile flatlines, almost becoming a grimace.

"Uh, what's he...?"

"Kerrim is the new Zodiac I mentioned," she deadpans.

Tristan visibly bristles, his posture stiffening and becoming defensive.

"Hi, everyone." Kerrim moves forward and gives a curt wave with one hand.

Tristan crosses his arms over his chest, scowling suspiciously at Kerrim. "I don't understand what's happening."

"Am I missing something?" Shreya asks, looking around from one face to the next with a big question mark in her gaze.

Tristan answers the question without removing his scowl

from Kerrim. "Apparently, the guy Brielle has been dating is a Zodiac. How do you know for sure?" When he flickers his eyes to Brielle, there's almost an accusation in them.

"Because I can do this." Kerrim lifts his hands and lets the same shadows slither through his fingers.

Tristan stumbles back, his eyes widening.

"Let me explain," Kerrim begins. "I am Prince of Araklya, the home world of the Scorpio sector. I'm the Scorpio Heir, and my father recently passed down the title of Guardian to me. He sent me here to Earth to find the lost Guardians, so that I might aid in the war with Chardis."

Tristan glances at Brielle, and she knows that look means he's asking her if Kerrim is telling the truth. Sensing no alarms from her lie detection, she nods. She can't believe this information herself.

"Your power isn't one I'm familiar with," Tristan says guardedly. "How do we know you are who you say? You could be an enemy. How do we know you're not in league with Chardis?"

Moving his hands up to his neck, Kerrim reaches under his shirt collar and pulls out a bright red ruby dangling from a thin chain. "Akash," he says, and from the gem, what looks like blazing dragon scales pixelate outward one over the other to encase his entire body in an impressive metallic red suit, flaunting the Scorpio symbol at the center of his breastplate.

Brielle hates that she can't help but admire the perfect way the smart metal frames his muscular stature, accentuating all of his strong curves.

"Okay, well he's definitely a Zodiac," Jareth says, a note of both awe and disappointment conflicting in his voice.

Tristan doesn't betray any form of surprise, just continues to scowl. "Then why didn't you come to us with this fact as soon as we met?"

Kerrim withdraws the suit back into his stone. "I couldn't be sure any of you were really who I was looking for. I had to be certain. Surely you must understand the need to protect my identity, just as you all do."

"He does have a point there," Logan says. "If he'd come out to the wrong people right from the start, that would've gone really badly for him. For all of us."

"So you preying on Brielle like a lamb ripe for the picking had nothing to do with your suspicions of who she might be?" Tristan snaps.

"Hey!" Brielle says defensively. While she had the same question, she doesn't like being made out to be so helpless.

"I sensed she might be a Zodiac, yes, which is why I wanted to get to know her," Kerrim retorts. "But I didn't expect to like her so much, or for the attraction to be mutual."

Tristan scoffs. "Please."

The last thing Brielle wanted was for this to turn into a testosterone contest between the two of them. "We don't need to argue about this. It happened how it happened, but ultimately, Kerrim's intentions seem to be...in the right place. He left his home planet to find us, to help us. And he's a Zodiac, so like it or not, he's part of our team. We're all in this fight together, and that's the only way we're going to win it. Together."

Tristan doesn't let up his suspicion, not that Brielle really expected him to. "That's another thing. I thought all of the heirs had been sent to Earth during the attack. Why didn't you?"

Kerrim nods, either oblivious to the bite in Tristan's tone or choosing to ignore it. "My family wasn't on the Space Station during that first attack. We had prior obligations that kept us from attending the Gemini birthing ceremony. After the attack, we decided to stick to our home planet and put all of our efforts into safeguarding our world. Chardis has destroyed so many of the Guardian planets."

Brielle sees Eric stiffen in the corner of her eye. They all just watched his home planet, Aqua, get annihilated. Kerrim's words hit home like a freight train.

Tristan doesn't miss a beat. "So your people decided to protect yourselves and forsake the rest of us?"

Kerrim shakes his head, the crease in his brow betraying his frustration. "No. We never stopped looking for the other heirs. But we couldn't be sure where you'd been sent. We've had scouts scouring every inch of the known Universe. It wasn't until recently that we became certain the heirs were even sent to Earth."

Tristan chews on his cheek as he considers Kerrim's responses.

Brielle no longer feels animosity toward Kerrim. There've been no alarm bells from anything he's said, and though she does feel a tinge manipulated, she doesn't know how else it could've happened.

No one says anything for a moment. They all just appraise Kerrim, keeping their thoughts to themselves.

"Wow, I had no idea there would be so much drama when I agreed to come here," Shreya says, and Brielle's surprised to hear amusement in her voice. Does she think this is a game?

"Shreya, I'm sorry, we didn't know this issue was going to come up when we brought you here," Ada apologizes, coming to her side.

Tristan's posture loosens as he seems to suddenly remember the other Zodiac in the room—and his obvious hopes for which one she might be. "Right, Shreya. We were just about to test you with the gems." He pauses on his way to get the case from its hiding place, looking over his shoulder at Kerrim. "Can you promise us that we can trust you?"

Kerrim flashes his sexy smile. "I swear on my throne that

I am here to help. I'm a Zodiac Guardian just like the rest of you. I want this war to be over just as much as you all do, and I won't rest until it is."

Tristan sighs. What other choice do they have but to trust Kerrim, and what reasons do they have not to? He's been raised with the full knowledge of who and what he is, and surely that knowledge can only help them. He's part of their team. They need him.

Without any further argument, Tristan retrieves the case containing the remaining gems. As he brings it before Shreya, the rest of the group gathers around them.

"Should we wait for Cassandra?" Brielle asks, noticing again that neither she nor Veronica are here.

"She hasn't responded to the alert," Ada says. "She'll just have to be informed later."

Brielle doesn't like that answer, but she can't see a reason to keep Shreya—and everyone else present—waiting any longer.

Tristan opens the case in front of the strange, pixie-like girl. "Which one calls to you? That will tell us which Zodiac you are."

Shreya looks down at the remaining gems, her eyes wide with anticipation. She doesn't waste any time in grabbing up the yellow topaz, and the stone emits a brilliant yellow glow that brings a jubilant smile to Shreya's face.

"Wow," Shreya gasps. "This feels amazing! Now what?" She looks up at all of them.

"Now say, Akash," Tristan instructs. "That will release your suit any time you need it."

"Akash," Shreya all but squeals with excitement, and soon she's encased from head to toe in a stylish daisy yellow suit that only makes her look more lithe, more petite, like their very own Tinker Bell.

Brielle can feel a sigh of relief escape her at the same time she sees Tristan's shoulders sag.

She's not the Gemini.

They have two new Zodiacs now. And yet, why doesn't Brielle feel happy about that?

CASSANDRA

Cassandra's alone in the dank basement, or wherever it is she's being held captive. Her ex-dad and Creepy Hat Guy left an hour or so ago—but then again, it's impossible to tell time down here. There are no windows or clock to speak of.

Though even if there were, she's too afraid to open her eyes.

The only way to keep the nightmarish hallucinations at bay is to keep her eyes squeezed tightly shut, all the while waiting and hoping for her friends to somehow find her.

Where are you guys?

The small *click*ing of creeping, crawling things sounds in stereo around her, but she ignores it.

There's nothing there. It's not real.

Something skitters up her bare arm, and she lets out a startled scream. But she refuses to look, knowing whatever she might see, whatever she might feel, isn't really happening.

Rage builds inside her, melting in with the venomous fear that the hallucinogen is pumping through her veins. How dare Richard do this to her! He really is the most evil man she's ever met—and she's come face-to-face with Chardis and Skins! She should've blasted him when she had the chance, but she was too drugged and overwhelmed with panic to react before he left.

She gasps, realizing suddenly that she *can* bust into her suit! It might help her escape her binds, and at the very least the use of it might signal the others as to her location.

"Akash," she whispers, her heart spiking with excitement.

But nothing happens.

Cocking her head curiously, she whispers the word again.

Still, nothing.

Why isn't her stone responding? Why can't she transform? Could it be possible that the drug they gave her dampens her Zodiac abilities?

Unless...

Taking in a deep, calming breath, she angles her head down and cracks open one eyelid to look down at her chest.

Then both eyes pop open with shock.

The stone isn't around her neck!

Balls! Richard took it!

Blinding fury boils throughout Cassandra's extremities, and she doesn't even care anymore what horrors still slither around her. She's *going* to get out of here, and when she does, she's going to kill him! Consequences be damned!

She looks around the room, blinking hard to try and separate reality from the hallucinations. She has to find a way out. She can't just sit around here and wait for the other Zodiacs to find her.

The room is made up of cement all the way around, except for the rafters of the ceiling above, which are made of wood. So, she's in a basement. But it's not the one at her old house—Richard's house. There are none of the familiar appliances, and the layout is totally different. Down here, there are only filing cabinets, all swarming with spiders, roaches and worms.

Not real. It's not real.

She has to keep telling herself this mantra to keep her pulse level, to keep the fear from paralyzing her any further than it already has.

To the far left corner is a cement staircase. That's where the two bastards left. She can't see the door at the top of it, but it must be there, and it appears to be the only way out. If she can just get out of this chair, she can get to the door and navigate her way through whatever lies above this hellhole.

With her arms tied behind her, she rubs her hands individually, priming them as she calls on her fire once more. They barely warm. Despite her intense anger, she can't make them light.

Dammit!

She closes her eyes and remembers every awful thing Richard ever did to her. Every time he beat her, every time he insulted and dismissed her. She remembers the day her so-called mom refused to believe her confession of who Richard really was, and the day they both kicked her out of the house.

Her hands burn hotter, but not enough to combust.

The fire that's always simmered inside her is far away. She can't reach it. All she feels is cold, the fear's icy touch saturating every part of her body and soul.

"Urgh!" she growls, squirming in her restraints in a fit of frustration. The rope rubs painfully against her bare arms, but she doesn't care.

Okay, so she can't use her powers, not even enough to trigger a dark matter signal to the others. But maybe she can call them! Her watch!

"Esther, can you hear me?"

Nothing but silence, and the imaginary pitter-patter, answer her call.

She cranes her neck over her shoulder to try and get a glimpse of her right arm, where the watch should be. She can't see anything under the tight ropes, but she realizes that she can't feel it there. The ropes should be pressing it against her skin, but she only feels the rope digging into her.

They took her watch, too. Does Richard know of its significance?

Hopefully not. Hopefully, he only removed it to better bind her wrists. Because if he does know, he can use it to trick the others, and she might never be found.

The heavy weight of resignation settles down on her, crushing her like a boulder.

She can't call for help, and she can't escape.

Not yet, anyway.

But this damned drug *will* wear off eventually, and when it does, she'll be able to burn her way out of here. Hell, burn this entire place to the ground and everyone in it.

She just hopes that happens before Richard comes back.

RICHARD

Richard paces the length of his home office. He'd hoped his… prisoner would've been more forthcoming, but then again, she's always been stubborn. Slow to learn. He shouldn't be surprised.

He'll just have to incentivize Cassandra sharing what's in that pretty, empty head of hers a little more. He knows how to break her. He's done it enough times before.

The door opens and a man slips in without knocking.

Richard's used to the man's ways, but it still grates. He's not accustomed to such a level of disrespect.

Then again, the man is a walking shadow, which is why he hired him. As long as he's useful, he's willing to tolerate his lack of social graces.

"Well?" asks Richard, keeping his voice low.

The man stops a few feet in, keeping the tip of his bowler's hat low over his eyes. "It's as we suspected. There are far more stakeholders after the book."

Richard narrows his eyes. "Do the FBI know of its existence?"

"Yes, Nebula is actively searching. I overheard a conversation between Solomon and Brielle. Jack Cadbury has the book."

Richard curses. "Then we relieve Cadbury of the book," he snaps.

The man in the hat nods once. "Consider it done."

He turns, about to slip back through the door as if he was never here when Richard speaks again. "And when we have the book, kill Solomon."

Another nod is the only acknowledgement the man heard, and then he's gone.

Richard picks up his phone, dialing with short, sharp movements. The receiver picks up after the first ring. "Yes?" says Senator Fitzgerald.

"We're retrieving the book," reports Richard. "It will be in our hands soon."

"Good," grunts Harrison. "And have you learned anything else about the Gemini Zodiacs?"

"Only that Tristan is one of them. We still don't know the identity of the second one." Richard's lips twist. "But I have someone who may be able to give me those answers."

"We don't have much time," warns Harrison. "Our master wants answers."

For the first time, a frisson of unease tickles Richard's spine. This is the greatest gamble of his life. The promise of untold power was too great to pass up.

But failure will mean death.

"I'll get the book and the answers," he promises coldly. His entire empire has been built on one motto—failure is not an option.

Senator Fitzgerald hangs up, and Richard quickly dials another number. This time, he's short and curt, the importance of success tightening his throat.

"Solomon. Find it."

11

BRIELLE

"This is seriously the coolest thing ever!" Shreya gushes, her voice muffled by her face shield. "What are my powers? Which Zodiac am I?"

Tristan is definitely deflated by the revelation that she's not the missing Gemini, and his sagging shoulders and facial features show it, as does his flat tone when he says, "Well, according to your stone, and the symbol engraved on your breastplate, you're the Sagittarius."

"So awesome!" Shreya squeals, her feet doing a little happy dance beneath her. "And my powers?"

Everyone looks to Tristan, who's deliberating.

"I can answer that," Kerrim interjects, taking a step forward. "I'm guessing things usually go your way? Every time you want something, it somehow finds its way to you? You frequently stumble upon dollar bills or get things for free from strangers?"

Brielle can't see Shreya's expression through her face shield, but she does nod ever so slightly, and for the first time since Brielle's met her, she's quiet.

Kerrim nods once, then clasps his hands behind his back

as he begins to pace. "Your power is a strange one. It's the only one among the Guardians that isn't offensive or defensive in any way." He turns to give Shreya a meaningful look, and the faces of everyone in the room are trained at him with anticipation. "In the bluntest language, you have the power of amplified luck. But more precisely, you automatically hack into all eventualities and are gifted with the most preferable outcome to you. It's very difficult for you to fail in any venture you set your mind to. Not impossible, just very unlikely."

Shreya's suit withdraws, and she walks up to Kerrim with awe in her wide hazel eyes. "So...what you're saying is I'm basically like Harry Potter when he takes the Felix Felicus potion?" Her eyes widen even more, and Brielle's chest squeezes slightly at how...cute she is.

Kerrim blinks at her several times, then shakes his head. "I'm sorry, I have no idea what that is. I've tried my best to acquaint myself with all of Earth's history and pop culture, but I'm not familiar with this. Who is this Harry Potter?"

Jareth snorts a muffled laugh. "I think you have some more studying to do, pal."

"I think your summation is correct, Shreya," Tristan says, a glint of excitement returning to his blue eyes. "And if that's the case, you might just be the most powerful weapon in our arsenal against Chardis."

"Yes. Your presence among the Zodiacs does tip the scales against Chardis quite a bit. It'll be harder for him to get one up on you now." Kerrim's tone sounds encouraging, and as Brielle can't keep her eyes off his handsome face, she sees a muscle in his jaw tick.

Tristan turns an appraising glance on Kerrim. "Your presence might've tipped the balance, too. You do seem to know more about the Zodiacs than I originally gave you credit for. What other knowledge can you share?"

Kerrim beams a bright smile. "Loads! Anything you want to know, but you'll have to be specific as I don't know where to start!"

The two of them fall into what Brielle is sure is a fascinating discussion of everything they don't know about the Universe, but she doesn't have the mental or emotional ability to absorb any of it, so she doesn't follow when they go off in a corner so Tristan and Ada can interrogate Kerrim.

She hates how relieved she is that Shreya isn't the other Gemini. She hates that she still can't fully let Tristan go. They're not together in any way, and there's no reason for him not to be happy with someone. And yet, that's the last thing she wants to see. And she hates herself for feeling that way!

Tristan deserves to be happy. And so does she. The best thing—for everyone—for the entire Universe—would be for the Gemini to show up already.

And the best thing she can do for now is ignore these feelings and will them into non-existence. She can start by welcoming their new member.

"I'm glad you're one of us," she says to Shreya, plastering on a smile. Fake it till you make it, right?

"Oh, me too!" Shreya says excitedly, her pink-tipped pixie hair bouncing as she does. "I knew there was something special about you as soon as I met you. And I knew we'd be best friends!"

She wraps Brielle in a surprise hug, and as Brielle recovers from the friendly assault, she has a feeling that Shreya's right. She's so cute and bubbly, the happiest person Brielle's ever met, and Brielle has to admit she's looking forward to getting to know her better. Besides, having a super lucky best friend definitely couldn't hurt. Maybe she'll spread some of that luck Brielle's way just by osmosis.

No sooner does Shreya release Brielle than Brielle's

phone buzzes in her pocket. "Oh, hang on, this might be Bea —ugh, my mom." She steps aside and pulls out her phone as Shreya attacks Eric with a hug, but Brielle's snicker deafens when she sees the number calling her reads as "Restricted."

There's only one person that could be.

While everyone is distracted, she slips out into the hallway, closes the door behind her, and answers the call.

"Hello?" she asks in a hushed voice.

"Brielle, this is Solomon."

Her eyes close as her suspicion is confirmed.

"Can we meet up?" he asks.

Brielle looks over her shoulder at the closed door of HQ. "Uh, now's not really a good time," she hedges.

"Okay, then I'll make this brief," he begins. "I have an idea how you can personally retrieve the book from Jack Cadbury."

Her ears prick at his words, her attention fully on his voice coming from the phone's speaker.

"I know that one of your compatriots is the hacker known as Dyad. Cadbury has been leading the investigation to find her. Offer him a trade. The book for the identity of Dyad."

"I can't do that," Brielle argues immediately. "I would never betray any of my friends—"

"The exchange doesn't have to be real," he interrupts before she can completely freak out. "I have a plan. But in order for it to work, we need to get Dyad in on it. But don't tell the others. This has to be just the two of you, that's the only way."

Brielle broods over this for a long moment. She still doesn't know if she can trust Solomon. Though she didn't sense a lie when he said he was shifting alliances, who's to say he won't shift again? His loyalty now means nothing if it won't be there tomorrow.

But she has to admit, she is interested in whatever plan he may have. If she can get the book from Jack, that will be a major win for them.

And it will make Tristan proud of her…

Ah pitch, why can't she stop thinking like that?

"Talk it over with Dyad," Solomon says after a moment of her silence. "When they agree, call me back and we'll go over the plan."

Before Brielle can say anything else, the line goes dead. She stuffs the phone back in her pocket, debating what to do next.

Ultimately, what's the harm in discussing this with Ada? Just because they consider Solomon's plan doesn't mean they need to act on it if it's not going to be favorable for them. And if there's a chance it really can get them the book, how can she not take it?

With a sigh, she spins on her heels and goes back into HQ.

Luckily, Ada is typing something on one of the many computers, and no one is paying her any mind as Shreya and Kerrim distract the others.

"Ada, can I talk to you in the hall for a moment?"

Ada turns her bright green eyes on Brielle with intrigue. "Uh, sure…" She gets up and follows Brielle out of the room.

After the whole fake-Gemini fiasco, the two of them don't have the strongest friendship, but Brielle can only hope that that doesn't inhibit Ada from trusting her in this endeavor.

And that this request doesn't blow up in Brielle's face.

12

SHREYA

Shreya has never felt this amazing in her entire life! Not only did she just learn her insane luck is actually a superpower, but because of it, she's now an integral part of a tight-knit group of friends that she somehow knows she'll never have to say goodbye to. No matter how many more times she moves or how far away life takes her, she will always be a Zodiac Guardian, and the others will always need her. She can't wait to get to know every single one of them!

"Come on, pick up, Cassandra," grumbles the muscular guy with sandy stubble framing his sharp jaw as he glares down at his cell phone.

She remembers hearing Brielle ask if they should wait for a girl named Cassandra. Could this be the same Cassandra she met at Creamy Dreams the other day?

Shreya decides to introduce herself to him. "Hi, it's Logan, right?"

He looks up from his phone and nods at her. "Uh, yeah. Shreya?"

"Yep! I heard you say the name Cassandra. Would she

few doors down. "Oh, and there he is!" he whispers hoarsely, and Shreya sees an older man approach the front door.

"Do you really think he would do something to her?" Shreya asks with a suddenly dry mouth.

The muscle on the side of Logan's jaw ticks, and he nods without looking at her. "There's no evil that man isn't capable of."

Shreya swallows, hoping her luck doesn't fail Cassandra. "Well, what are we waiting for? Let's go!"

Logan slides her a skeptical side-long glance. "How does this whole luck thing usually work?"

She shrugs. "Well, not like I've ever been on a mission to possibly rescue someone before. But I usually just wing it, and things end up working out."

"So, you have no plan?" Logan asks.

Shreya looks at him blankly for a moment, not really understanding what's up with the scrutiny in his eyes. "I find things usually work better for me if I don't plan. Just trust me."

"Okay," he says on a sigh, then follows her out of the car and toward the house Cassandra's dead-beat dad just went into.

Honestly, it's not like she's going to go right up to him and say, "Yo, have you seen Cassandra? She was stalking you earlier, and we're pretty sure you caught and kidnapped her. Do you have her locked up in some creepy basement or something?"

She snickers at the absurdity of it as she leads the way in a leisurely stroll across the road like she's just out for an evening walk. When she said she didn't have a plan, she meant she had more of a loose idea of what she was intending to do, and right now that's basically snoop around the house until an opportunity presents itself. Plans are too rigid and don't allow flexibility for the random circumstance or errors, and they've just never worked out for her.

The streetlights illuminate the front yard, creating starkly contrasted shadows for them to disappear into. Shreya walks down the side of the house with her hands in her jacket pockets, not necessarily trying to stay hidden, just acting casual. She figures it'll make it easier to claim she's looking for a lost dog or something should anyone question what she's doing if they catch her. The easiest way to be invisible is to not try to hide.

A man's voice carries out an open window, and Shreya leans up against the wall of the house beside it to listen, nodding her head to Logan for him to do the same. He clearly looks uncomfortable at following her, like he wants to sneak up against the wall or tiptoe over the grass. What are they teaching in FBI school these days?

"What is it now?" the man barks inside, and the lack of a response makes Shreya sure he's talking on the phone. "Ugh, I don't have time for this. The drugs will wear off soon, and we need to get information out of her before that happens. Or at least get another dose in her."

Drugs? Information? Is he talking about Cassandra?

Heavy footsteps pace inside, moving away from the window, as Cassandra's dad allows whoever's on the other line to talk. "Can't you deal with it on your own?"

Another beat of silence, and Shreya looks over her shoulder at Logan, whose face has gone from tense to murderous. If she wasn't sure this conversation was about Cassandra, Logan sure seems to be.

"Ugh, very well. I'll be right there." The call ends with a subtle *beep* and a frustrated grumble.

"What is it, darling?" a woman asks, assumedly Cassandra's deadbeat mom, her voice sounding further away. The kitchen, perhaps.

He clears his throat. "Oh, uh… There's been a problem at work. I have to go deal with the incompetence of others."

"Aw, that's too bad. When will you be back?" she asks, her tone sounding bored.

"Hopefully within an hour." His footsteps move toward the front door. "Oh, and don't go into the basement. We have a pest problem. I'll be bringing an associate to help me take care of it." Without a pause for her acknowledgment, the front door opens and closes.

Shreya and Logan wait for the sound of a car rolling down the driveway and speeding down the road.

"She's in the basement," they whisper to each other at the same time.

"How are we going to get her out?" Logan asks.

"It's just her mom here." She sneaks a look into the window and glimpses the petite woman, who's sipping on a glass of wine at the kitchen island as she stares down at her cell phone. "We can take her. She's tiny."

Logan frowns, then his eyes spark. "I've got a better idea. I'll be right back."

Adopting her casual posture and stride, he goes back to his car, opens the trunk and pulls out two plain gray jackets that resemble custodian attire. She eyes him as he returns and hands her one before donning his own. "You'd be surprised how often these come in handy for undercover work."

"What are we doing?" she asks, shrugging into the jacket and zipping it up.

He raises a sly eyebrow, the corner of his mouth tipping up. Damn, all these Zodiac guys are seriously hot! "He said they have a pest problem."

Her mouth spreads in a wide, excited grin. Holy crap, is she actually going to go undercover? This is awesome!

Logan leads the way to the front door, and Shreya

follows, trying not to look like a kid in a candy store. He rings the doorbell, and soon the petite bird of a woman opens the door, wine glass in a manicured hand.

"Yes?" she asks, eyeing them up and down.

"Pest control, ma'am," Logan replies, pushing past her in an all-business way.

"Uh, my husband said you'd be here in an hour with him," Cassandra's mom says in an irritated, prudish tone.

"Well, our six o'clock job got canceled, so we had an opening now," Logan says.

She purses her lips like a duck as she considers them for a moment.

Logan sighs. "Look, I'm eager to get home to my girl. Can we get this taken care of quickly?"

The woman rolls her eyes. "Fine. It's in the basement. Just...don't touch anything you don't have to."

Logan nods at her, then pauses. "Er, your necklace!"

At his outburst, Shreya notices the stunning yellow gem that hangs from a fine chain around her neck. It's roughly the same size as her own stone.

Cassandra's mom rushes a hand to it, running her fingers over it. "Yes, my husband gave it to me as a gift."

"It's truly beautiful," Shreya praises. "He has fine taste."

"That he does." She smiles, feigning flattering for an instant before the irritation crawls back over her features. "Well, get to work." She waves them away before returning to her post at the counter and downing another long sip of her wine.

Logan grabs Shreya's wrist and pulls her out of sight, then whispers, "That's Cassandra's citrine. That's why she hasn't been able to get away. She can't use her suit. And they have her drugged with something. We have to get it back."

Shreya nods. "Okay." She sneaks her head around the

corner of the wall to peek into the kitchen. The stone glints in the recessed lighting overhead.

Suddenly, the necklace slips off Cassandra's mom's neck and clatters on the countertop.

"What the..." The bird woman picks it up and wraps the chain back around her neck, but with her inebriated fingers, she can't clasp it into place. With a huff, she sets it back down on the counter and puts her attention back on her wine glass and phone.

Acting on impulse, Shreya strides into the kitchen and heads for the sink. When the woman glances at her suspiciously, Shreya offers, "It's a real mess in there," then rolls up her sleeves to wash her hands.

The woman ignores her as if pretending she's not there will make it true, and Shreya continues with the ruse, letting the water spill over her hands. She needs a distraction. How is she going to get Cassandra's mom away from the necklace?

Before she can come up with anything, a high-pitched sneeze sounds behind her, followed by an outraged, "Ah, dammit!"

Shreya turns around to see that the sneeze caused Cassandra's mom to spill her wine, dark red liquid saturating into her very white blouse. She rushes past Shreya to fetch the hand towel from the rack, patting her chest to no avail, then huffs again as she storms away, probably to change.

Without wasting another second, Shreya snatches the necklace from the counter and hastens back to the hallway where she left Logan. "I got it, but we have to get out fast before she notices it's missing," she whispers.

Logan nods and leads the way to the basement door. He grabs the handle, but it doesn't turn. It's locked. Shreya opens her mouth to ask what their next move is, but Logan is already pulling a paperclip from his pocket and jimmying it into the keyhole. It clicks with ease, making Shreya's racing heart jump for joy.

They open the door and rush down the stairs.

The gorgeous, fierce blond girl she met at Creamy Dreams is tied to a chair, ropes binding her chest, wrists and ankles.

Cassandra lets out a shriek as they approach, squirming away from them in a terror that Shreya doesn't understand.

"Cassandra, it's me, Logan," he says soothingly, his puzzled expression matching Shreya's confusion. Shouldn't she be relieved they've come to rescue her?

"W-what? Logan?" Cassandra blinks up at him several times. "Is that really you?"

"Yes, we're here to get you home," he reassures.

"And…you brought a demonic fairy with you?" She stares at Shreya with horrified eyes.

Demonic fairy? What the heck?

"Uh, I'm Shreya," Shreya offers. "I'm new to the gang. Long story, no time." She bends down to work away at the ropes binding Cassandra's legs, and Cassandra flinches.

"Baby, what's gotten into you?" Logan asks as he unties the ropes around Cassandra's torso.

"I—he—they drugged me with something," Cassandra stammers, shaking her head and squeezing her eyes shut. She looks nothing like the fierce, bold girl from the fro-yo shop. She looks frazzled and vulnerable. "A hallucinogen or something. It's somehow dampened my powers…" Her eyes pop open. "And my stone! They took my stone!"

"It's okay," Shreya shushes, getting the first leg free and turning to the second. "I've got it back. As long as we make it out of here before anyone comes down, we should be good."

Cassandra doesn't look convinced, a deep crease between her spectacular eyebrows. "I… Are you sure this is really happening?"

Logan presses a lasting kiss to her forehead. "I promise this is real." He rips the loosened rope away from her and pulls her to her feet as Shreya gets the last one free. "Now, let's get out of here."

Cassandra's throat bobs as she nods and lets them pull her to the stairs. "I swear, I'm going to kill him for doing this to me," she vows murderously.

"I'll hold him down when you do," Logan promises.

"And I'll stand by to make sure neither of you gets caught," Shreya adds as they make it to the top of the stairs.

"I'm sorry, who are you again?" Cassandra asks as they step into the hallway.

"She's the Sagittarius," Logan explains. "She just joined our team before we came to look for you."

"I'm basically a walking rabbit's foot," Shreya supplies with a shrug.

"What?" Cassandra asks, but she's silenced with a *shush* from Logan as he looks down the hallway for Cassandra's mom.

They all freeze, looking around and listening. The sound of running water carries from one of the bedrooms where Shreya guesses the bird-like woman is fretfully washing her soiled shirt in the master bathroom.

"We're good," she whispers. "Let's go."

They tiptoe on quick feet to the front door and amazingly make it out of the house right before Cassandra's mom comes storming down the hall with a huff that's cut off by the closing of the door.

Logan lets out a heavy breath. "That was amazing!" He gawks at Shreya with awe. "You really are our good luck charm! The way you got that necklace—"

"Less talking, more getting the hell away from here," Cassandra snaps, jerking him off the porch.

Shreya beams as she follows them back to Logan's car.

She just completed her first successful rescue mission. She can't believe this is her life now! And she has no doubt that, with her help, they're totally going to save the Universe.

Chardis, you better watch your back!

BEATRICE

Bea taps her fingers impatiently on the steering wheel, as if that will make time go faster. She glances at the car clock for the hundredth time, letting out a frustrated sigh when the numbers haven't changed.

"Not long now," she murmurs to herself.

When the passenger door opens, Bea turns to the person climbing in her car, bracing herself. Some good news would be nice. "What do I need to know?"

Olivia arches a brow as she settles into the leather seat. "I suspect you organized this meeting here and now because you're well aware of what I have to tell you."

"I was hoping you'd surprise me," Bea says, uneasiness slithering amongst the broken shards of edginess already there.

Olivia shakes her head. "Everybody is searching for the book."

Bea nods as she lets out a breath. Through the windscreen the large, gray building squats morosely, surrounded by twelve-foot fences, watching them as closely as she's watching it. "Brielle's in danger, isn't she?"

"She is," says Olivia, now also gazing out. The leader of Operation Castle adjusts her loose bun almost unconsciously, as if she's preparing herself for something. "Others will try and take advantage of her."

Because Bea's daughter is so sweet. All Brielle does is see the good in people. All she wants is for others to be happy.

Olivia turns to her. "And we know she's in contact with a guy who once held the Staff."

The uneasiness is quickly chased away by alarm. When Bea and Frank joined the Operation, they'd welcomed the suggestion they adopt Brielle. They'd always wanted children. But they hadn't realized exactly what a perfect fit Brielle would be. That she'd make them a family. Now, they've gained a daughter, and they'll protect her at any cost.

"What do I need to do?" Bea asks, the words as soft as they are fierce.

"Keep her away from the Staff," says Olivia. "It's too dangerous."

And the book has the location of the Staff. "Consider it done," Bea promises.

Olivia leaves in the same way she came—no greeting, no acknowledgement this meeting ever occurred. Bea lets out a pent-up breath. At least she won't be doing this on her own.

As if her thought triggered it, the monstrous gates jolt into motion, slowly scraping open. Bea springs out of the car and breaks into a run, tears already wetting her cheeks as she crosses the parking lot.

Frank's tall frame appears in the gap created by the rolling gates. Even framed by chain-link fencing topped with loops of barbed wire, wearing a t-shirt that hangs loosely after losing a few pounds, he looks like heaven. He opens his arms and she runs straight into them, gripping him with everything she has.

"I missed you," she sniffs.

"It's so good to hold you," he says, burying his face in her hair and breathing deeply. He pulls back. "What did Olivia say?"

Bea sighs, then relays the brief meeting in the car he

knew was happening. His tired face tightens with each word. When she's done, Frank slips an arm around her shoulder and they make their way to their car. So they can go home.

"The Zodiacs can't get their hands on that book," says Bea, her arm clamped around his waist.

He nods resolutely. The need to protect their daughter is stamped as clearly on his face as it is on her heart. "Then we get hold of it before they do."

13

TRISTAN

"How is she?" Tristan asks Logan as he walks back into HQ.

Logan sits heavily in the nearest desk chair. "The nanites are working their magic."

Tristan nods, the image of Cassandra when they brought her in still fresh in his mind. Battered, disorientated, and clinging to Logan in a way he's never seen their strong Leo do. When Logan had told Tristan where they'd found her—in the basement of her own adoptive father's house—he'd understood the fury etched in his friend's stoic face. Cassandra was tortured by the man who hurt her all her life. The man who should've been her protector.

It only emphasized the need for the Zodiacs to be that for each other.

Guilt gnaws at Tristan's mind and he shifts his weight where he's perched on the end of his desk. They should've checked on her sooner, which is one of the reasons he's called this meeting.

"I wanted to discuss something," says Tristan, scanning each face scattered around the room. Everyone's here apart from Cassandra, Ada, and Brielle. Jareth sits not far away, Veronica standing beside him with a hand on his shoulder. Eric is also standing, his arms crossed as he waits intently. Logan leans forward, his elbows on his knees as he clasps his hands. Shreya's gaze is bouncing around everyone as she registers the intensity in the room.

Oh, and then there's *him*. Kerrim stands to Tristan's right, as if he belongs in this circle. Which he technically does. Kerrim's the Scorpio. The thought has a sour taste tainting Tristan's tongue. It never occurred to him that he would struggle to accept a Zodiac. But that's exactly what happened when it was revealed Kerrim was one of them. In fact, he's not sure he trusts the guy, and that leaves him in one heck of a difficult position. The Zodiacs will only succeed if they're a team.

He shakes away the disturbing thoughts. Everyone is going to assume it's nothing more than jealousy. And a little part of him worries they're right. "It turns out we have more enemies than just Chardis and his Skins, meaning Esther won't always be able to warn us of changes in dark matter. From now on, if a Code Red is issued, please reply. If I don't receive anything within a few minutes, I'll contact you."

"As will I," echoes Esther through the speakers.

Everyone nods, no doubt having already thought this themselves. It's what they should've done with Cassandra in the first place.

Kerrim clears his throat. "We should also talk about the book and getting it back."

"Ah, sure," says Tristan, his gaze not quite making contact with him before sliding away. "It's our only link to the Ark."

"Actually, it has directions to the Staff."

Tristan's gaze shoots straight back. "The Staff?"

Kerrim's dark eyes glint like the smug bastard he is. "Actually, to the two pieces of the Staff. The parts have each been hidden in a different location to protect it. The book is the only place those locations are recorded."

Jareth leans forward. "We need that book more than ever then."

"We most certainly do," agrees Kerrim. "The Staff is the only thing that can channel the power needed to destroy Chardis."

"Wow," Eric mutters.

Kerrim's gaze falls on Tristan. "The Gemini twins are going to need it."

Tristan's jaw clenches at the double blow. Kerrim obviously knows more about the book and the Staff than he does. And he's just reminded everyone in the room that Tristan has a soulmate out there, waiting for him.

He drags his gaze away. "Then we need to get the book from Jack." He sighs. "The guy who isn't answering my calls."

Veronica's face twists. "I'm not sure he really wants to talk to you or any of the Zodiacs right now."

Logan nods. "And there's the alliance to consider."

The fragile agreement Tristan and Jack reached that they leave each other alone. It's the only thing that's kept Nebula off their backs.

"And we're not handing Ada over with some crazy scheme to get her back," adds Eric, steel laced through his voice.

"Agreed," says Tristan, watching his friend visibly relax. "We don't sacrifice one of our own."

"Let's hope Jack hasn't figured out the book has the locations of the Staff pieces," Kerrim points out.

"Pitch," Jareth mutters. "That's the last thing we want."

A vein somewhere in Tristan's temple twitches with the start of a headache. They need to decide what their next step is.

Kerrim shrugs a shoulder. "I say we break into Nebula and get it back."

Silence hangs in HQ as everyone digests this. If they do that, then the truce with Jack is kaput. Then again, what other choice do they have?

"We need to talk this over with everyone," Tristan says, sliding a glance at Kerrim. "We work as a team here."

Kerrim simply nods. "I can try and call Brielle?"

"I'll do it," he snaps back. The only reason he can stomach having Kerrim here in the first place is because he's obviously not with Brielle. If the two of them were standing like Jareth and Veronica are—always close, always touching—he's not sure what he'd do.

But a few punches of his screen later and all Tristan gets is her voicemail. A second call yields the same results. Pitch.

"I'll try, just in case," Kerrim says smoothly.

He dials then holds his cell to his ear. "Hey, Bri. Yeah, I'm just at HQ. Whatcha doin'?"

Tristan's teeth jam so hard into each other he wonders how they don't crumble.

"Oh, your dad's out of jail? That's great news. We were just talking about the book. We're thinking we might go get that sucker back."

Kerrim nods, keeping his gaze focused on the floor even though everyone can hear the conversation.

"So you won't be back till later? All cool, you focus on family. We'll see you then."

He hangs up and turns to Tristan, and he swears he sees a glint of triumph on his non-committal face. "She's with her parents. Said she won't be back here till tomorrow. I didn't want to push it."

"Very considerate of you," says Tristan through his clenched jaw. Personally, he would've given Brielle the choice.

"We can do this without her," says Kerrim as he tucks his cell back in his pocket, still pretending that getting hold of Brielle was no big deal. "We probably don't want too many of us going in, anyway."

Tristan looks away, wishing there's some way he could argue any of this, but knowing he'll just come across as jealous and petty. He's never minded anyone else taking the reins or calling the shots. Just like he wouldn't have minded anyone else calling Brielle…

He swallows any words of objection, then turns to Eric. "What about Ada? We could use her skills to get us into Nebula."

"Ada told me earlier she's nose-deep in code trying to see if she can triangulate the location of the Ark," he replies. "But I can get us in."

"So, we're doing this?" Tristan asks, scanning the others.

"We need that book," Kerrim says resolutely. "So I'm in."

A slow procession of nods circles the room. Tristan doesn't bother to join in, seeing as it's a majority vote. He would've liked Brielle and Ada here before they'd finalized anything, but once again, he doesn't want to seem oppositional. Right now, the Zodiacs need unity.

Plus, he probably is nothing more than jealous. Brielle answering Kerrim's call stings more than he'd like it to.

Logan pushes to his feet. "I'll check on Cassandra. My guess is she's not going to want to miss this."

"Good idea," says Kerrim before Tristan can speak. "The nanites would've taken care of her injuries by now, and we could use her firepower."

Logan glances at Tristan, but when he doesn't say anything, he jogs up the stairs to the first floor.

Shreya blinks as she looks around. "So we're going to break into Nebula?" she asks, the only one here looking like she's actually excited. "Like, now?"

Tristan pushes away from the desk he's leaning on. This happened a little fast, even for him. "No time like the present, it seems."

Kerrim claps his hands and rubs them together. "We get the book, we find the Staff."

14

BRIELLE

"I hope this works," Brielle says softly as she and Solomon walk up to the inconspicuous brick building on the outskirts of Manhattan. There's no sign or lettering of any kind to give this building any kind of identity, and everything about the façade says, "Go away, nothing to see here."

The prospect of failing has Brielle's pulse jackknifing. They need the book. Plus, now that Frank's home and their family are finally reunited, the last thing her adoptive parents need is a phone call saying Brielle's been arrested. Or worse.

"It'll work," comes Ada's voice over the speaker in Brielle's ear, and she knows Solomon can hear it from his, too.

"Just as long as we have him convinced, that's all that matters," Solomon says, then pauses before they open the front door and glances at Brielle. "You ready?"

Brielle lets out a shaky breath and nods once.

"We got this," Ada says through the earpiece.

Brielle envies Ada's seemingly never-ending confidence. She wishes she could feel so self-assured before walking into a top-secret, government-sponsored organization with a plan that will probably go south. Although, not that Ada technically is the one walking in here, but she's just as much at risk.

After all, she's the one the FBI truly wants.

The inside is a small, plain white room with one brown door behind an L-shaped counter where a young female clerk sits just beyond a computer screen. There's nothing else in this room but a pair of very basic, unimpressive metal office chairs against the right wall and a dismal-looking fern against the other.

The clerk—or whatever she is—braids her fingers on the countertop in front of her and smiles. "Can I help you?"

Brielle does a visual sweep of the room, feeling awkward. "Er, we have a meeting with Jack Cadbury?" Her statement turns into a question on its way out.

The woman looks them up and down and Brielle holds her breath. Solomon said everything was organized. Her face neutral, the woman raises a pointed index finger as she picks up the black rotary phone. "Sir, a young woman and a gentleman are here to see you."

Brielle glances at Solomon while they wait for the response. Her hands are sweaty, so she clandestinely wipes her palms on her jeans at her sides. Too bad she can't do the same for the sweat under her arms. She can only hope the colorful paisley blouse she's wearing doesn't show pit stains.

The woman sets the phone down and rises, heading for the ominous door behind her. "Right this way," she says to them with that same clinical smile.

Brielle and Solomon follow. *What the heck is this place?*

On the other side of the door, the clerk leads them down a hallway lined with more doors. They walk all the way down, and Brielle is very uncomfortable with the depth in which they're now trapped in this building. If something goes wrong, they have a long way to run, and possibly a lot of obstacles to evade judging by the number of doors they've passed. Who knows how many agents or whatever are working inside.

At the final door, the clerk knocks twice, then heads back up the hallway, leaving them alone. *Yeah, that's encouraging.*

Soon after, the door opens, and there stands Jack Cadbury, five o'clock shadow firmly in place around his tight features. He gives them a long look over.

"Where's Dyad?" he asks in a flat tone.

Solomon steps forward, and Brielle feels her neck bob as she swallows. "Right here."

Jack arches a skeptical brow. "*You're* Dyad?" His tone is dripping with disdain.

"I am," Solomon vows.

Jack sighs. "You expect me to believe that you're the criminal computer mastermind behind the digital heists over the past five years?"

Solomon offers a smug grin. "I can prove it."

Jack stares at him for a long moment, considering. Finally he steps aside, a silent invitation for them to come in, and rounds the expensive wooden desk to sit opposite them.

He leans back in his chair as they sit down, crossing his arms over his chest. "Let's say you are Dyad. Why would you be willing to trade yourself in so that a wayward bunch of teenagers can have a dusty old book?"

Solomon crosses his arms as well, and when he speaks, his southern drawl is sharper than usual. "Let's be frank here, Cadbury. You and I both know that this 'wayward bunch' are no ordinary teenagers. And you and I both know that the book in your possession is no run-of-the-mill text. It is my hope and belief that, by working together, we can achieve the one thing that is most important to all of us."

Jack purses his lips. "And what's that?"

Solomon opens his arms, the gesture smothered in his southern charm. "Why, world peace, of course!"

"And you think the book can accomplish that?" Jack prods.

"I do, indeed." Solomon nods.

Jack leans forward on his elbows. "Alright. How about that proof you mentioned?"

Solomon quirks his head at an angle. "I'm gonna need to see that book first."

A muscle ticks in Jack's jaw before he bends down, and a round of subtle *beeps* tells Brielle that he's entering numbers into a safe of some sort. He returns upright and gingerly places a large, ancient tome on the desk. It's so thick, and the binding is covered in strange yet beautiful embossed symbols in some glimmering metallic material. The auspicious sight takes Brielle's breath away.

"Very well," Solomon agrees.

Ada's voice sounds in Brielle's ear, spouting out a slew of words about code and crypto currency and other stuff that Brielle can't begin to understand. It might as well be Chinese to her. Solomon repeats every single word in a very matter-of-fact tone, and honestly, hearing him say it, she'd think he is truly the expert he claims to be.

Jack then asks very specific questions about a number of crimes committed by Dyad, and Ada feeds Solomon detailed information that only the perpetrator could know—or comprehend.

With each response, the skepticism on Jack's face receded little by little. *This might actually work!*

Suddenly, there's a loud crash from the hallway behind them.

Brielle and Solomon spin around, and Jack shoots up out of his chair. "What the—"

Before he can finish the question, the door flies off its hinges, and a man in a brown bowler hat storms in. In the hall behind him, handfuls of men are fighting each other, and Brielle has no idea which side they're on.

"What's going on?" Ada asks in her ear, but Brielle refuses to answer in front of Jack.

"You," Solomon hisses at the hatted man.

The man's eyes flick from him to the book on the table, and he lunges for it. Jack pulls out his gun at the same time Solomon tackles the hatted man, and Jack is left aiming and waiting for the opportune moment to shoot.

But the melee in the hall is increasing. Brielle looks around the small office, then to Jack.

"Is there another way out?" she asks.

"They're not with you?" he snaps at her, indecision wrinkling his features.

She makes a flabbergasted expression. "Does it look like they are?" She doesn't even know who they are. They're not Skins. Skins would've been stealthier than this. And…she just doesn't sense that emptiness in them. She can taste all of their guilt on the tip of her tongue.

"Please, we have to get the book out of here before they can take it by force," she urges, desperation coursing through her panicked limbs.

Jack visibly gulps. "The only way out is through there." He nods at the narrow hallway that is littering with tangled bodies. "This location was supposed to be secure. No one knew about our new headquarters after we left the FBI building." He tossed her an accusing look. "They must've followed you here."

Or Solomon…

More bodies burst into the hallway, but this time—

They're in suits!

It's the other Zodiacs!

"What the hell are *they* doing here?" Jack accuses Brielle, now clutching the book tight against his chest.

"I—" Brielle is almost too stunned to speak. "I really don't know." How did they know to come here? She didn't tell any of them. Did Ada? Maybe she told Eric and he ratted them out.

The fight comes flooding forward, and soon Jack's office is a maelstrom of slamming fists and flying fireballs.

"Brielle, what's happened?" Ada asks again, this time in a much firmer tone.

"The Zodiacs are here," Brielle shouts over the bustle.

"No shit!" Jack barks as an assailant lunges at him. On reflex, he drops the book to raise his gun and shoots his attacker square in the forehead.

The book! But before Brielle can go for it, her legs are pulled out from under her, and she slams face-first onto the linoleum.

Ouch!

She struggles to roll onto her back to return the fight, but a wonderfully familiar figure in a platinum purple suit pulls her attacker away.

"Brielle? What are you doing here?" Tristan's muffled voice hisses in surprise.

This time, she's too stunned to speak, to do anything but shake her head.

Not that her answer would've mattered as the hatted man and Solomon fall on top of them in their epic battle. The hatted man's hand stretches out for the book, only inches away. As Tristan and Solomon continue to wrestle with him, climbing over her.

"Jack!" Brielle calls desperately, but when she looks in his direction, he's out cold on the floor. *Oh no!* Is he dead?

In a sudden twist, Solomon fists the side of the hatted man's face and rams it into the floor, knocking him out, then scrambles over his body to grab the book.

15

TRISTAN

Tristan manages to stay silent the whole drive back to the house, even if it means developing lockjaw. In fact, keeping his mouth clamped shut is the only way he knows to stop himself from exploding.

How could Brielle keep something like this from him? Solomon, of all people!

They've lost the book! Their one link to the Ark, and apparently to the Staff!

All because the one person Tristan thought he could trust went rogue.

His hands practically strangle the steering wheel as he pulls into the driveway, the other Zodiacs all silent including Brielle, who's tucked in the corner of the backseat. So many questions are punching through his mind, but one hits the hardest.

How could she?

Tristan carefully opens the front door, leaving it that way for the others to enter as he stalks to the secret entrance to HQ. He counts each step on the way down, hoping it will calm him down. He makes his way to his desk, planting his

"Brielle!" The sultry voice belongs to Kerrim, and she sees his red suited figure above her, offering her a helping hand.

She takes it and lets him pull her up, excitement filling her that they have the book at last!

Except...when she turns back to look at Solomon, he's no longer hovering above Jack's body. She frantically turns her head around to find the tail of his coat flapping just beyond the doorway—as he makes a run for it.

"No!" Brielle shouts. She looks back at Kerrim. "The book!" She points at the hallway, but Solomon is already gone, having leapt over bodies and weaved through brawls to escape with their only chance of defeating Chardis.

How could she be so stupid to trust him?

fists on it and lowering his head, focusing on nothing but his breath the way Zarius taught him.

And none of it helps.

The moment he hears each of the Zodiacs enter, he spins around, his words bursting out of him like a backed-up bazooka. "What the pitch happened back there?"

Everyone is silent. Disappointment in the outcome of their mission has the couples—Jareth and Veronica, Cassandra and Logan, Eric and Ada—all standing close, their frowns mirroring each other. Even Shreya's perma-smile has slipped away. Turns out her luck didn't make a difference in getting the book.

Tristan tries not to let his gaze settle on Brielle, but the weight of what she did makes it too hard to do otherwise. She crosses her arms and raises her chin, a contrasting show of defensiveness and defiance that seems to both tug at his heart and inflame the frustration.

"Solomon contacted me," she says, her voice quiet but steady. "He said he'd only work with me. I thought it was our only chance to get the book."

"And you agreed," Tristan grinds out.

"I knew the book was important." She holds his gaze. "I wanted to help."

"Well, you didn't!" he snaps before he thinks. "We've lost the book, Brielle!"

She winces as she ducks her head. "I know. I'm sorry."

He wipes his hand down his face, trying to get his emotions under control. He's doing everything Zarius taught him not to—acting without thinking. But even as his good intentions try to take the reins, more words slip out. "I thought you trusted me."

Brielle's second wince is even more pronounced as her head tucks into her shoulders. "I—"

"She said she's sorry," says Kerrim, stepping forward.

Tristan's eyes narrow at him. "Stay out of this."

But he doesn't look away. "Solomon is a master manipulator. One who's been obsessed with the Staff since he once held a piece of it. You need to back off, she made a mistake."

The frustration quickly morphs to anger, heating and hardening all at once. "No, you need to back off. You're new, so I'll let this slide. The Zodiacs work as a team."

"Really?" Kerrim drawls. "Cause it sounds like you're talking for all of us right now."

"Stop it!" Brielle cries, looking horrified as her gaze bounces between the two of them. She looks like she's about to say something, but her face crumples. Tristan takes an involuntary step toward her, but she spins on her heel and runs out of the room.

Tristan follows as far as the base of the stairs, then stops, torn. He spends long seconds staring at the empty doorway at the top of the stairs, wondering how things seem to be unraveling so fast. Behind him, he hears Logan clear his throat. There's a barely perceptible shuffle from Jareth's direction. Then a very subtle, but undeniable, snort from Kerrim.

The emotions storming through Tristan feel just as out of control as everything else.

"I'm going for a run," he says, not looking over his shoulder. He doesn't need to see Cassandra's frown or Shreya's confused face. He's feeling all that and more.

Silence chases him up the stairs, and it's only once he's reached the top that he realizes something else.

The truce with Jack has been shot to hell.

JACK

16:35

Jack steps over the dead body of one of his men, his gut clenching. Each of the agents he lost today were loyal to Nebula. To the fight to keep Earth safe from the threat of aliens.

And they died for that cause.

They died because of the Zodiacs.

The clean-up crew move through Jack's office with quiet efficiency, the thick plastic of the body bags being unwrapped the only noise in the room. It allows Jack the space to consider his next steps, seeing as he'll never trust the Zodiacs again. There will never be another truce.

He yanks his cell phone out of his pocket. "Davies, I want two tails on Logan and Veronica."

He hangs up with a sharp jab of his finger on the screen. He's humored his children's association with the Zodiacs long enough. Now he has irrefutable proof they can't be trusted.

And that they're dangerous. The dead bodies being swallowed by black plastic is evidence enough.

It's only a matter of time before he ensures Logan and Veronica never have anything to do with the Zodiacs again.

16

SHREYA

A beautiful sherbet glow colors the sky beyond the windows as Shreya rides the bus home. Her mind is so full of conflicting emotions that she's not sure how to feel. So much has happened in the past twenty-four hours.

She found out she's a frickin' superhero, which is totally the most amazing thing that's ever happened to her! She's thrilled about that!

Then she had her first successful rescue mission saving Cassandra from her twisted adopted father's wrath. Also awesome!

But then there were the events of today. They'd been on their way to the FBI building, where Tristan said Nebula was located in plain sight. On their way there, Shreya had this nagging feeling in her gut pulling her in a different direction. Tristan had been determined to follow his directions, but Logan had stood up for her and encouraged them to go where she led.

Luckily enough, they'd stumbled blindly onto the right location, where a fight had already broken out. Tristan had no idea the Nebula HQ had moved. She felt great being able to help, and certain her presence would ensure they get this book they're all looking for.

And yet, it slipped right through their fingers. Her gift of luck had failed. She'd never read about that in Harry Potter. She can't help but feel like she let everyone down. Maybe it would've made a difference if she'd been able to contribute to the fight, rather than standing back like a fly on the wall because she has no combat training yet—one thing Tristan insisted needs to be rectified immediately and her training will begin tomorrow.

Despite the high she's been riding since her induction as a Zodiac, she doesn't think she's ever felt more...bummed. She's honestly never failed at anything before. She's always gotten good grades, always succeeded in school and sports, always won at card and board games, except for when it was her intention to lose. Maybe if she had wanted the book itself more, rather than just wanting to be a part of this new team, they wouldn't have lost it.

It's her fault.

She sighs.

"Hey there." A guy with a large, fancy camera hanging around his neck suddenly takes the empty seat beside her. "What's a pretty girl like you frowning for?"

"Huh?" She looks up at him. He's wearing a pink polo, and from the tone of his voice and choice of wardrobe, he's clearly not into women.

He flashes her a flamboyant smile. "You have to be the cutest thing I've seen in this town in, like, ever. Your hair," he reaches up to flick one of her pink-tipped spikes, "truly stunning. You have to tell me who did your look, 'cause it's to die for!"

"Oh, um," Shreya stammers, caught off guard by the compliment, but it does instantly lighten her mood. "I did it myself."

The guy's jaw drops and he gasps. "No! You have a keen eye for fashion!" He grips his camera and lifts it up. "I would *love* to shoot you for an upcoming gallery in the city. The theme is Nitty, Gritty and Pretty, and you'd be perfect for it!"

Excitement bubbles through her chest, and she can't help but feel like her luck is back on her side. "Sure, I'd love to!"

He claps his hands in a short and fast gesture. "Yay! Do you have time now? The lighting is great, and there's a really cool underpass just ahead with graffiti that would go perfectly with your look."

Shreya purses her lips and looks at the time on the flashing sign at the front of the bus. It's only five-o-five. She has time before her parents are expecting her home, and she has to admit that the setting sun is offering a great ambiance. They can probably get in a few shots before nightfall.

"Yeah, I got time." She shrugs. "Why not?"

"OMG, I love you *so much*!" he gushes. "Okay, let's get off at the next stop. The underpass isn't far from there." He bounces next to her. "You have totally made my night!"

His eyes, though bright, have a slight silver ring around the irises. Odd, she's seen something like that before. Maybe it's a new contacts trend?

Shreya follows him off the bus when it comes to a stop at the park crossing. He picks up the pace, waving her after him. "Come on, we have to get these in before the streetlights come on."

She runs after him at a brisk pace, eager to see this underpass he mentioned. She hasn't noticed much graffiti in this suburb, and she's excited to see it. She's somewhat of a fan of street art. Even if the majority of it is often gang-related, she's seen true masterpieces throughout the country done by people who just use walls as their chosen canvas, and though she has no artistic talent to speak of, she greatly admires such passion.

After a jog through an industrial neighborhood and over a railroad track, she sees the underpass just ahead, and the graffiti does not disappoint. Giant letters she can't fully read painted in brilliant shades of red, orange and yellow with undertones of black and brown. The orange glow of the sky makes it shine in the shadows, and she can already picture the photographs of herself leaning against the vandalized concrete.

When they get to it, he grips her shoulders and places her where he wants her, then takes a few steps back to aim with his camera.

"Yes, just like that," he says. "These will be great!"

Suddenly, strong hands grip her arms from behind, and the cameraman lowers his camera, his flamboyant expression abandoned and replaced with a smug look of victory.

"What-what's going on?" she stammers as she looks back and forth between the two large men who've taken hold of her.

"Not so lucky, after all, are you?" says the guy who brought her here, a taunting lilt to his voice.

Lucky? What?

With a sudden thump deep in her belly, as if her heart has just plummeted through her torso like a dead weight, Shreya realizes what's happened.

Skins.

She's fallen for another one of their tricks! Holy crap! And that last girl who tricked her out into the alley, she'd had the same silver-rimmed irises! That's where she'd seen them before.

How could she be so stupid?

The cameraman flicks his eyes up to her captors. "Get rid of her, quickly, before her powers can come into play. Chardis will be pleased to know she's been eliminated."

At the command, the men drag Shreya backward, and she

screams, "Help! Someo—" But before she can get any more pleas out, a hand clamps over her mouth, silencing her. She tries to jerk out of their hold, but they're far too strong, and she's too petite. It's like a twig trying to shove a boulder.

Panic grips her as she realizes this is the end. She foolishly walked right into a trap, and no one is coming to help. Her luck really has run out.

A scuffle behind Shreya precedes the hands restraining her being roughly and abruptly yanked from her arms, and she falls flat on her butt. After recovering from the jarring sensation, she scrambles around to see a well-built guy with a buzzcut taking on her attackers and kicking some serious butt. Both men are bigger than him, but he uses stealth and speed and tactics she's only seen in movies to subdue them both.

There's clatter in the other direction, and she turns to see the camera broken on the ground and its owner making a run for it several yards away.

Only once both men are knocked unconscious does her savior turn his attention to her. "Are you alright?" He offers her a calloused hand, and she takes it with overflowing gratitude.

"Yeah, I'm fine, thanks to you." She dusts off her ripped jeans, all the while appraising her rescuer with her eyes.

The word "rugged" is blaring in her mind. This guy is chiseled. And hot AF! He's wearing camo cargo pants, and a dog tag hangs around his neck, resting on his plain white t-shirt. Military. That explains his expert combat skills.

"No offense, but what were you doing out here with those guys?" he asks, his scrutiny making her heart stutter.

"I, er." She points a thumb over her shoulder in the direction the camera dude fled. "That guy said he wanted to shoot me for a gallery." Now that she says the words out loud, she realizes how stupid they sound.

Her rescuer arches a dumb-founded brow. "Hold on. So you followed some random stranger to an abandoned underpass because he said he wanted to take your picture?"

She tries to hide the frown that's setting in. "Well, yeah. It sounded like fun." Even though she pushes as much confidence into her tone as she can muster, she knows she doesn't have a leg to stand on in this argument.

"Were you raised under a rock or something?" he accuses, crossing his buff arms over his impressive chest. "Don't you know how messed up people can be? Didn't your mother ever tell you not to talk to strangers? Much less follow them into shady ass places?"

"No," she says snidely. And it's the truth. She's spent her entire life talking to strangers. She's never had a reason not to trust people. She realizes now that, as a Zodiac Guardian and apparently the number-one target of the evilest dude in the Universe, she'd better start being more cautious. Suspicion has never been in her vocabulary. It needs to be.

He shakes his head in frustration. "Well, seeing as you clearly can't be left out here alone, where's your home? I'll escort you."

She opens her mouth to object, but falters. She really doesn't feel safe being out here by herself. There could be more Skins around here ready to catch her off guard. And honestly, she's never been one to refuse the aid of a hot guy.

"Fine," she grinds out. "If you insist, you can walk me to the bus station. I can take it from there without your help."

He eyes her for a moment, unconvinced, then nods. "Fine by me."

She spins on her heel and walks back toward the bus stop, hearing him following behind. Despite her deep mortification at this guy's obvious opinion of her ineptitude—and knowing full well it's justified—she feels safe in his presence. There's something about his aura that makes her want to slow down and shorten the distance between them, but her wounded pride refuses to let her legs reduce their stride.

They make it to the bus stop, and luckily, the next bus is coming just down the street.

"Well, here we are," she says, chewing her lip. "Thanks. For, you know, saving me back there."

"Sure thing," he clips, but at her exposed vulnerability, he seems to soften. His lip quirks in an almost grin. "What kind of a soldier would I be if I didn't help a damsel in distress?"

"Uh, yeah." She rubs the back of her neck awkwardly, actually wishing that the bus wasn't getting closer. "Let's just hope I don't need you again." Crap, why did she say that?

He nods, his lips flattening into a straight line again.

The bus pulls up, and the doors slide open. She plants one leg on the first step, then looks back at him. "Hey, what's your name, by the way?"

He'd begun to stroll away, but stops and looks over his shoulder. "Ethan. Ethan Hunt."

She offers him a grateful smile. "Thanks, Ethan."

He returns her smile, and her heart does a somersault in her chest. "Any time." He winks before continuing down the sidewalk with his hands in his pockets.

She completes the climb onto the bus and takes the first available seat. As the bus rolls forward, she's again conflicted. She just got mugged and humiliated in front of the hottest guy she's ever met. But she doesn't feel terrible.

This whole luck thing is tricky, but maybe being lured into a trap wasn't so unlucky after all.

17

TRISTAN

Tristan stops beside his bed, his breathing still accelerated from his run despite the long, hot shower he just had. He roughly towel dries his hair before looping it over his bare shoulders, even his low-slung tracksuit pants feeling a little too warm. He'd just about lapped Mirror Point, he'd run that long. He's not sure how many hours he was out, but streetlights illuminated his way home and the house had been silent as he'd crept in.

He glances at his bed, conscious it's getting late. He should get some sleep.

But he knows he won't be falling asleep easily with the same certainty that he knows today's consequences will be far reaching. With the book gone, they have no way to find the Ark or the Staff.

Tristan stretches out on his bed and stares at the ceiling, absentmindedly tracing the outline of the sunken lights. Despite the Zodiac team having the most members since the search began, he feels far more alone than he ever has. He always imagined it would get easier the more Zodiacs they found. That victory would feel so much closer.

But everything's just so...complicated. Logan and Veronica are the children of Jack Cadbury, the head of Nebula. Cassandra's father knows of the Zodiacs and would go as far as torturing his own adopted daughter to find out what he can. And now Brielle's not talking to him...

Thanks to Kerrim.

Tristan knows it's not rational to blame it all on the new Scorpio, but he can't shake it. He doesn't trust him.

Jealous, hisses a voice through his mind. *All when you have a soulmate out there, waiting for you.*

Tristan rolls over with a groan, punching his pillow as if it's at fault, then promptly rolling onto his back again. He won't be getting to sleep anytime soon, even if the last thing he needs is to be tired. Tomorrow is coming at him whether he likes it or not, and they have to figure out how to get the book from Solomon. Wherever the lying douche is.

Even as he wonders if he should just get up and surf the net for mentions of pods or aliens or some other desperate search for a lead, Tristan doesn't move. His body rebels at the thought of doing anything. It wants rest, even if his brain isn't in agreement.

He sighs. It's moments like this he misses his parents the most. Zarius would've said it was obvious he needs to work Tristan harder the next day, but Tessa would've brought him hot chocolate. Of course, it was the worst tasting hot choco-late ever because she'd lace it with chamomile tea, but Tristan always drank it. Always. He knew how lucky he was to have them as his parents, both barely old enough to be called that when he was a baby.

Their love for him was as unwavering as their determination to find the Zodiacs and defeat Chardis. He'd drink a million hot chocolate-chamomile mixers just to see them again.

A soft knock on his door interrupts his sad musings and

Tristan glances at his watch. It's after ten, who would be paying him a late-night visit?

Yanking on a shirt he opens the door, stilling as he registers who's on the other side. "Brielle?"

A smile ghosts over her lips. "Hey, can we talk?"

Tristan blinks, wondering if his mind has finally snapped and he's hallucinating. He steps back, opening the door a little wider. "Sure. Come in."

To his surprise, she enters and walks straight over to his bed and sits down. She tucks her hands beneath her thighs and he can't help but notice the way the sleeve of her top slips from her shoulder. He wipes his hand down his face, telling himself to get a grip.

She looks up at him, that fragile smile back. "I thought we should talk."

Tristan closes the door then wonders where he's supposed to move to. There was a time when he would've given in to the tug in the gut and sat beside her on the bed without a second thought. But that time is gone. He and Brielle aren't together. She's with Kerrim.

Clearing his throat, he leans back against the door, goes to cross his arms and then stops. "Look, I was frustrated earlier—"

Brielle raises her hand, stopping him. "You have a right to be angry. I should never have trusted Solomon."

"I think I was just..." Betrayed. "Frustrated."

"I only wanted to help." Tristan grits his teeth as she echoes what Kerrim said. Even if it's the truth. "He told me the Staff could harm a Gemini."

Tristan frowns as he moves closer. He realizes how little they know about this Staff. "Do you think he was telling the truth?"

Brielle shrugs. "I don't know. There are other things he told me that were the truth, like that the book was more important than we realized." She tucks her hands further under her legs. "I really am sorry."

"I know," he says on a sigh, finding he's now standing beside his desk chair. It's the closest he'll let himself get to Brielle. The two of them, alone, in his room, is playing havoc with all the memories of when they were together.

Up in the attic. Kissing.

In her room. Kissing.

Them kissing. Period.

He suppresses a groan as he wipes his hand down his face. "It'll work out. We'll get the book back, somehow."

Brielle nods, chewing her lip. She watches him for excruciatingly long seconds, her green gaze inscrutable in a way he hasn't come across before. They've drifted farther apart than he realized.

"You look tired," she observes quietly.

"Yeah," he says, even though it's an understatement. He's freaking exhausted.

She pats the bed. "You should get some rest."

Her words shock him into stillness. It was only a handful of hours ago that she ran out of the room looking like she was about to cry. And now she's inviting him to sit next to him? On his *bed*?

She shuffles further down and pulls back the covers. "I don't like us fighting," she says softly.

Neither does he.

Unwilling—possibly unable—to say no, Tristan sits on the bed, a couple of feet between them. He wonders if she can hear his heart thudding in his chest. He wants to tell Brielle he's missed her. Missed this.

Missed *them*.

But he stays silent, not wanting to break whatever's happening here.

Brielle rolls her eyes. "Lie down, silly. Even you wouldn't sleep sitting up."

Tristan does as he's told, tucking his legs around her and stretching out with his head on the pillow. He barely breathes as she pulls the covers up and her hand hovers near his shoulder.

"Sleep, Tristan," she murmurs, brushing a lock back from his forehead. His eyes flutter closed at the caress as he breathes in deeply, absentmindedly noting she's changed her shampoo brand as his eyes flutter closed. Sleep wraps around him in the same way contentment is, and he willingly gives into it.

"I'll protect you from the Staff, I promise."

Despite the odd words, Tristan sinks further into the mattress. He has no idea what brought on her change of heart, but he has no intention of questioning it. This is the closest they've been in months.

As his muscles unwind far more than he remembered possible, he admits this is the most peace he's felt since their breakup. Since he wanted to tell her how he feels. The bed shifts as Brielle stands, and her soft footsteps and the sound of the door gently opening and closing are the last things he hears.

If things are okay with Brielle, then everything else will fall into place.

He just knows it.

18

KERRIM

Kerrim walks out of Tristan's room and gently closes the door behind him, not wanting to disturb the gentle mood he's just put Tristan in. He softly pads to the bathroom, making sure no one's in the hall to see him. He can't be spotted like this.

Sure that the coast is clear, he goes in and locks the door. He smiles smugly at the mirror over the sink, enjoying the way this expression looks on Brielle's pretty face staring back at him. She's so sweet and mild, he's never seen more than a frown settle on her features.

Kerrim can't believe it worked. After the way Brielle stormed out, Tristan still bought that she would come to comfort him even after he'd publicly scolded and berated her. But then, he's an easy mark. Tristan won't admit it, to himself or anyone else—least of all Brielle—but he's so desperate for her favor that it makes him weak. Easy to manipulate. As Brielle, Kerrim could've asked Tristan to jump off a bridge, and he's fairly certain that Tristan wouldn't think twice before leaping to his death.

That could work, actually.

Brielle's reflection smirks as Kerrim lets out a chuckle. Then, calling on the shadows, they swirl around Brielle's face as the features morph back into his own, birth-given one.

"You handsome devil," he purrs at himself, flashing his reflection a wink. Nothing to do now but chill on the couch and watch how the chips fall tomorrow morning.

His sleep on the recliner is a restful one. Sure, he could've gone home—or to his current earthly residence, anyway—but he doesn't want to miss any of the action. The furniture of this unevolved anthropoid species is crude at best, nothing like the smart fabric of his home world that instantly adjusts to the pressure needs of the occupant based on musculature and bone structure, but it's not the worst accommodations he's ever made do with.

When his father first tasked him with coming to Earth, Kerrim had imagined a slightly more primitive society. Perhaps evolved enough to live in huts, or to have possibly discovered little more than steam power. He was actually impressed with their level of technology, but his expectations had been fairly low, so that wasn't saying much.

That had been years ago, and he's become accustomed to this planet's ways over the few trips he's made.

He's eager to finish his task, get off this rock and return home before the big finale.

The purpose his father was born, and had raised him for all his life.

The Zodiacs may think they're doing the right thing fighting on the wrong side of this war, but they don't understand the vision his father has. One of purification, not just for the living, but for the balance of the entire Universe.

He cannot fail. And after how easy things have been so far, he's confident he won't. These Zodiacs are like wet clay —soft, malleable. Easily squished. It's only a matter of time.

The sound of chatter and the heady aroma of the strange

brown morning liquid these humans like to consume—coffee?—rouse Kerrim from his peaceful slumber. Some of the Zodiacs are bustling in the kitchen. Kerrim sits up on the recliner, hoping he hasn't missed too much. He enters the kitchen to see who's here.

Jareth is at the coffee maker, and Tristan is leaning against the counter looking quite content and well-rested.

"'Morning," Jareth greets before sipping from his steaming mug that reads "World's Best Boyfriend". "I saw that you slept on the couch. You know, we have spare rooms available if—"

Kerrim stops him with a wave of his hand. "Nah, won't be necessary. I was just too tired after yesterday to go home, and I didn't want to impose."

Jareth pushes another steaming mug across the counter at him. "No imposition, at all. You're one of us. What's ours is yours."

Kerrim smiles, glancing dubiously down at the dark liquid. Its smell is appealing, but the idea of ingesting anything the color of mud, of filth, turns his stomach, so he decides to ignore the mug altogether. "Thanks."

"Good morning!" Veronica trills as she comes through the front door. She skips into the kitchen and places a brown paper bag on the counter before pecking Jareth on the cheek. "I brought bagels!" Then she opens the fridge and pulls out a red can, popping it open.

Cola. What is it with these human and brown drinks?

"Is Brielle around?" Kerrim asks the group.

At the mention of Brielle, Tristan wakes from whatever daydream he was entertaining and looks up at Kerrim.

"No, I'm pretty sure she has to work this morning," Tristan says, then adopts a smug expression. "You two work together, shouldn't you know that?"

"Tristan," Veronica hisses, but Kerrim is unruffled.

"Ah, yes, that's right," Kerrim remarks. "I think I'll go have a morning treat, then."

Tristan pushes away from the counter, a challenge in his blue gaze. "I'll go with you."

"But I brought bagels," Veronica complains, holding up the bag.

"Thanks, they'll make a great lunch," Tristan says before heading out of the kitchen.

Kerrim is quick on Tristan's heels, the two of them practically racing for the front door. And down the driveway. And all the way down the road to Creamy Dreams. Kerrim isn't the least bit winded keeping pace with Tristan, and it fills him with satisfaction to see Tristan so flustered in this way. And to know it's his doing.

Reaching the frozen yogurt shop, Tristan shoots Kerrim a glare as they approach the door, but Kerrim lets him go in first, wanting to appear the bigger man. Plus, he wants a front row seat to what's about to happen.

At the dinging of the bell over the shop's door, Brielle looks up. That deepest frown Kerrim's ever seen her make weighs down her features, and she quickly busies herself with wiping the counter.

"Hey," Tristan calls as he approaches her. He folds his elbows over the counter and leans against it. "How are you?"

Her brow raises, but she doesn't look up from her needless cleaning. "Fine," she says in a clipped tone.

Tristan's posture stiffens, defensive. "Uh, is something wrong?" he hedges, the airy note his voice previously held deflating.

Brielle stops her wiping and looks up at him, deadpan. "What do you think?"

"Well, uh, wh—" He glances over his shoulder at Kerrim, who raises a daring brow at him, then he returns to facing

Brielle and rubs the back of his neck. "After last night, I thought we were cool again."

Brielle glares at Tristan. "Really? After you scolded me in front of everyone and made me feel like a traitor and a fool, you thought we were 'cool'?"

"No, I mean—" Tristan stammers.

Brielle slaps the cloth down on the counter and huffs at him. "Are you going to buy something or not? Because if you're not, I'd like to help the next customer."

Tristan looks around at the empty shop, seeing only her, him and Kerrim. Kerrim waves his fingers at both of them and flashes a friendly grin.

Looking defeated and confused, Tristan backs away from the counter, stumbling into one of the empty tables and upsetting a napkin container. "Okay. Guess I'll see you later." Then he turns around and stalks past Kerrim without so much as a glare in his direction.

The doorbell rings again to declare his departure, and Kerrim strides up to the counter to claim his victory. "What was that about?" He nods over his shoulder.

Brielle shakes her head and huffs again. "I honestly have no idea. He can be so dang clueless sometimes."

Kerrim adopts a pout. "I'm sorry. Can I take you out after your shift, and help you forget about him?"

She flashes a scrutinizing glance up at him, looking like she's going to refuse. But then her shoulders lower, and she sighs, perhaps choosing one poison over another. "Sure. I could use the distraction." She intensifies her gaze. "And some answers."

He nods and smiles. "Your wish is my command." He pats the counter and pushes back. "I'll pick you up here at two."

"Don't be late," she calls, a hint of tease in her would-be stern tone.

"I wouldn't dream of it."

He strolls out of the shop and takes in a deep breath of the crisp autumn air. The sun is shining, the birds are chirping, and everything is working out perfectly.

The Zodiacs are so clueless. How did his father ever think they were a threat?

JACK

10:47

Jack surveys the old barber shop Davies asked him to meet at. Judging by the boarded-up windows and the smashed barber pole, it closed down some years ago. Which means it's abandoned. Secluded. Private.

And that concerns him.

There can only be one explanation as to why his agent asked to meet Jack in a place no one will hear them—Logan and Veronica are more deeply involved with the Zodiacs than he'd like.

Jack reaches into the pocket of his suit jacket and pulls out a strip of antacids and pops two out. He grinds the gritty, pasty tablets between his teeth and swallows, hoping they work fast. His stomach feels like a churning inferno.

All because he suspects his kids' loyalty is elsewhere. Veronica is head over heels with that Jareth guy, and Logan's been distant. Not to mention he keeps saying he can't find anything on Tristan and the others.

Which is bull.

Tristan and the others are Zodiacs. Jack would bet the curing of his ulcer on it.

Logan and Veronica obviously have no idea what they're getting mixed up with, or how dangerous it is. They're leaving Jack with no choice. Their safety will always come first.

His decision to have his children removed from the influence of the Zodiacs only further cemented, he tries the door to the barber shop and isn't surprised to find the doorknob twisting in his palm. He slips in and quietly shuts it behind him.

Jack squints as his eyes take a few seconds to adjust to the gloom of the old shop. Thin rays of light squeeze through the sheets of wood nailed to the large windows, revealing a place outfitted like a barber in the 60's. There are three gas-lift chairs to his left, a mirror stretched along the wall, all coated with a thick layer of dust. Davies is sitting in the chair furthest away, his back to Jack.

"Davies," he says, striding in. "What have you got?"

But two steps are all it takes for Jack to register the agent's face in the mirror in front of him. His head lolls to the side, his mouth lax. A neat, round bullet wound punctures his chest, a bloom of blood surrounding it.

Davies is dead.

Jack spins around, realizing this was a trap, only to freeze all over again.

A row of men appear, one by one, blinking into existence and blocking the exit.

Aliens.

Jack reaches into his jacket for his gun, but the men move fast. One leaps forward and powers his fist through Jack's chin. Another catches him before he can stagger backward. A third grabs his other arm, immobilizing him.

Jack fights with every shred of strength he has, but the grips on his arms are like a vice. And then the alien on his right jerks his knee up, slamming it into Jack's solar plexus. He doubles over, now half-hanging from the hands holding him as his breath is replaced by pain. It takes long seconds for his seized lungs to function again, and when they do, Jack finds himself once more upright, his arms painfully pulled taut as if he's about to be crucified.

The alien who struck his jaw steps in close, a scowl twisting his features. "Where's the book?"

"I don't have it," snaps Jack, hating that it's the truth.

"Liar," the man growls. "Tell us now and you'll save yourself a whole lot of pain and disfigurement."

Jack tries to think fast. The thought of torture isn't palatable. The thought of pointless torture because he doesn't have what they want is downright ulcer-growing. If he can get out of the barber shop, he may have a chance.

The slap that has his face snapping to the side cuts off any wild plans of escape. The next one that has his head jolting back the other way has his ears ringing. He's still blinking away the rattle to his brain when the uppercut slices through his chin. Jack groans as his knees give out once more and he's left hanging like wet laundry off his captor's grip.

Rather than push up, which will no doubt mean more immediate violence, he sags where he is, trying to keep his wits about him. They think he has the book, which means they need him alive.

Unless their patience runs out…

The door slamming against the wall has his captors startling, which instantly gets Jack's attention. They have visitors. Ones the aliens weren't expecting.

Men in navy blue paramilitary uniforms rush in, guns ready. Jack makes the most of the surprise entrance, yanking his arms free. He reaches for his gun, but it's all over before he's withdrawn it.

Several muffled gunshots fill the barber shop and the aliens drop in quick succession, now graced with a discrete hole in their forehead.

Jack's harsh breathing fills the sudden silence and he

raises his own gun even though he knows it's useless. These men are professionals. He's only standing here alive because they let him.

No doubt because they also want the book.

Two of the men step aside and a woman walks through. Dressed in smart slacks and a neat gray blazer, her hair softly frames her face in a loose bun. She walks straight up to Jack, acting as if she doesn't have to navigate several dead bodies and is unaffected by the gun he still has raised.

She extends her hand, a congenial smile on her pleasant face. "Hello, Jack. My name is Olivia Wilde. Lovely to meet you."

19

JARETH

"This was a good idea," Jareth says as he glances down at Veronica.

She smiles as she wraps herself a little tighter around his arm, the afternoon sun catching in her chestnut waves. "You were about to turn into a tangled ball of nerves," she teases lightly. "I figured a walk would do you good."

He presses a soft kiss to her head, breathing in the crisp scent of citrus and coconut. "You were right."

Straightening, he lets Veronica take the lead as they wander the streets of Mirror Point. His mom firmly believed people need both purposeful time and time with no purpose whatsoever in their lives. That it was during those moments where the mind recharges, free of shoulds and coulds and have-tos.

She was also right.

They take a right and tuck in closer as a guy jogs past, a panting German shepherd by his side, complete with a camera strapped around its chest. The man nods politely and they nod back.

The moment he's out of ear shot, a giggle escapes Veronica. "It's not just Google that's always watching."

Jareth grins as he shakes his head. But then he sobers as he thinks of how long Tristan was gone last night, also for a jog. They're not supposed to go out alone anymore, not since what happened to Cassandra. And yet, the backbone of the Zodiacs went for a punishing run well into the night. Jareth hadn't breathed easy until he heard the front door open and close.

"Jareth?" Veronica asks, frowning a little.

No longer surprised at how in tune she is to his emotions, he allows the truth to tumble from his lips. "I'm worried about Tristan."

"Yeah. What sane person rejects free bagels?"

"He's trying really hard to keep it together, but there's so much going on."

She arches a knowing brow. "Zodiac-wise or Brielle-wise?"

Jareth sighs, withdrawing his arm from her clasp so he can wrap it around her shoulders. Some days, he can't pull her in close enough. "Both." They reach the end of the block and Veronica keeps going straight ahead. "And then there's Brielle herself. She wants so much to do her part. I don't think she realizes it's Tristan's approval she's seeking."

Veronica scrunches up her face. "Even though she's with Kerrim."

This sigh is deeper. Longer. "So complicated." He rubs the ache that's developing in his temple. "I'm worried about Cassandra, too. Being tortured is bad enough, but by the only man you've called your father? That's gotta leave scars on multiple levels."

"You're a good friend, Jareth." Veronica squeezes his waist. "You're worried because you care."

He almost smiles at that. "My mom used to say that."

Veronica's brown eyes twinkle up at him. "Great minds, huh?"

Jareth can't help himself, he presses a soft, tender kiss on her lips. Just like she always does, Veronica melts into him in the most delicious way. Their mouths mold to each other, the action now familiar, yet gloriously breathtaking each and every time.

Veronica somehow has his heart soaring and grounds him, all at once. Just by being her.

They pull apart, smiling tenderly at each other, memories of all their moments together melding with the promises of all the ones they're yet to make.

Veronica peeks around him. "We're here."

Jareth turns, realizing he was so lost in thought, and Veronica, that he hadn't realized she had a destination in mind. His eyebrows shoot up when he discovers where they are.

A small park is tucked among the suburban houses, a climbing gym with a plastic slide in the center. But that's not what has a delighted smile climbing up his lips.

The lawn surrounding the gym hasn't been cut for a few weeks, and white daisies dot the dark green like stars.

Veronica presses against his side as she rests a hand on his chest. "Our flower."

His arms instinctively wrap around her. "Our flower," he whispers. He looks down, his heart feeling the size of the Universe itself. "I love you."

"I love you, too," she says huskily.

A harsh voice interrupts their sweet moment. "You're a threat, and you know what I do with those, Cassandra."

Jareth and Veronica pull away in shock. They turn in the direction of the angry tones, registering two people standing beneath a tree on the other side of the park. Richard Sinclair.

And Cassandra.

"Actually, you don't know what *I* do with threats," she says, flicking her mane of hair over her shoulder.

Jareth and Veronica glance at each other, concern passing between them.

"We should back her up," says Veronica.

He nods. "Before she does something she regrets." Their Leo is as fiery as she is determined.

They move simultaneously, using long strides to cut across the park.

Richard takes an ominous step toward Cassandra. "Don't think that just because you asked to meet me in a public place, I won't punish you again."

"You will never hurt me again," Cassandra snarls, extending her hands palm out.

"Cassandra!" Jareth cries out in alarm as they break into a run.

Veronica gasps. "Surely she won't—"

Light explodes from Cassandra's palms, spearing across the few feet between her and her father and straight into Richard's chest.

The force thrusts him backward and he slams into the tree. The sickening crack of his head against the trunk is undeniable even at a distance, making Jareth's stomach turn.

Richard slumps to the ground, unmoving.

Surely Cassandra hasn't…

She looks over her shoulder as they approach, either unsurprised or unconcerned that Jareth and Veronica are here. "I've been wanting to do that for a long time."

Jareth comes to a stop, breathing as if he just ran from the other side of the city. He tries to comprehend what he's looking at. It's as if this is exactly what Cassandra intended to do, damn the consequences.

Veronica squats down beside Richard, her fingers pressing against his neck. A moment later her shoulders slump. She looks up at Jareth, her gaze heavy. She doesn't speak, but she doesn't need to.

Richard Sinclair is dead.

And Cassandra killed him.

She lifts a defiant chin. "He deserved it."

Jareth gapes as Veronica gasps again. Surely Cassandra must realize what she's done.

"We're not killers, Cassandra!" Jareth works to modulate his tone, shock and anger clashing inside him. "And we're out in the open!"

The last thing the Zodiacs need is more publicity. Especially a cold-blooded murder.

Cassandra's eyes flash. "I don't care." She glances down at her father's still-warm corpse and curls her lip. "I have no regrets."

She spins so fast her hair furls out, then stalks away.

"She's lost it," Veronica mutters under her breath.

She really has. Jareth looks back at the dead body they're now standing beside. "We have to tell Tristan." The torture has broken Cassandra far more than they could've imagined.

Jareth lifts his hand, preparing to create the illusion of a pile of leaves and debris to hide Richard's body until they can figure out their next steps, when another gasp echoes.

One that didn't come from Veronica.

They turn to the sound as one, Jareth's heart leaping into his throat. What he sees instantly has his head swimming. Panic constricts his chest, making it hard to breathe. He grips Veronica's hand, needing her anchor now more than ever.

The jogger they passed earlier is disappearing down the street, running as if he's trying to break the sound barrier, his dog beside him.

The dog with the camera strapped to it.

SOLOMON

The park bench creaks softly as Solomon stretches out his legs, enjoying what's left of the afternoon warmth. A smile hovers on his lips and he savors that, too.

Everything is falling into place.

It's only a matter of time before he'll have his revenge.

"What is it with you and this park?" says a voice behind him.

Solomon doesn't move or look up as Frank Pierce settles next to him. He shrugs. "I've learned to enjoy the simple things in life."

Facing death so many times does that.

Frank clasps his hands, no doubt trying to hide his tension but failing dismally. "Do you have it?"

"Of course I do," Solomon says, mildly insulted. "I promised you I would."

"Well?"

"Not much for enjoying the view, are you?" When Frank just stares at him with the same intensity vibrating through his body, Solomon chuckles. "Here. You'll need to wipe water over the pages to see the text. The hydrogen reacts with the ink."

He reaches into the satchel tucked on his other side and passes the item to him.

Frank takes the book, allowing himself a brief second to run his hand over the embossed symbols glittering softly on the cover. Alien symbols. A language only those not from this world can decipher. Then he tucks it into the backpack he brought and zips it up.

He rests a hand on it as if he doesn't intend on letting it out of his sight. "The Zodiacs can never get their hands on the Staff," he says, his voice low and intense.

Solomon inclines his head. "Well, you have the book now, ensuring exactly that."

Frank gazes out at the park, letting out a slow breath. "I'm grateful. You've ensured the safety of more people than you realize."

"It was my pleasure," Solomon says, meaning it.

Although admittedly, not in the way Frank would be thinking.

The well-meaning man smiles as he pushes to his feet. "You're right." He tucks the backpack to his front, almost hugging it to him. "This place is nice."

Solomon's gaze falls on the variegated lawn and tranquil trees. "Yes, it is."

He doesn't watch Frank walk away, although he's acutely aware of the man's movements. Once he's out of sight, Solomon silently counts out five minutes. Frank would've made it to the parking lot by then, probably sooner thanks to the urgent need to hide the book somewhere no one will ever find it. He's no doubt already calling Beatrice with the good news.

Solomon withdraws his cell from the satchel and taps the screen, making his own phone call. "Meet me at Central Park on the eastern side of the lake. I have something you want."

He hangs up without waiting for a response. The person on the other line will come. He guarantees it.

Solomon once more stretches out his legs as he draws in what no doubt looks like a long, peaceful breath. He even allows the small smile to return. In some ways, he is at peace.

He's finally going to have what he's worked so hard for.

Soon Chardis will pay for what he did to him.

20

BRIELLE

It's been a long day, and it's only two o'clock. Brielle sighs as she pulls the apron over her head and hangs it on the wall. At least she has a lunch date with Kerrim to take her mind off things.

No sooner does she step out the front door of Creamy Dreams than her phone rings in her back pocket. She hopes it's not Kerrim calling to cancel. But when she pulls it out, the screen reads *Restricted*.

Her heart jumps into her throat, making it difficult to swallow. Whoever it is, it can't be good.

She answers it anyway. "Hello?"

"Meet me at Central Park on the eastern side of the lake," says an oddly deep voice, one that is clearly being modified. "I have something you want."

Before Brielle can ask anything, the line goes dead, and she's left standing there practically choking on the lump in her throat. What the pitch just happened? Who was that? And what could they possibly have that she wants?

Unless…

The hunch burns all up and down her esophagus, leaving

a sour taste in her mouth. Would she be absolutely insane to go? Certainly not alone. But who could she take with her? Ada's in the doghouse with Eric already for the stunt they pulled at Nebula, and everyone else has lost their faith in her. Especially Tristan. She can't go rogue again, but she can't ask anyone to go with her, and she can't *not* go.

There is Kerrim, who's supposed to meet up with her anyway. He did stand up for her when Tristan scolded her in front of everyone. But she has a very distinct feeling she shouldn't involve him. He may not have outright lied to her, but he did withhold information from her for a long time to gain her trust, which is almost as bad.

"Hi, Brielle!" The lithe body of Shreya presses against her torso in a surprise hug before Brielle can register the greeting. She pulls back just enough to offer Brielle a friendly grin. "I just had the sudden desire to pay you a visit! I'm not too clear on this whole luck thing, but I had a feeling you might need my help, so I just went with it."

Relief fills Brielle's chest like a fresh gust of wind. "Shreya, I could kiss you right now!"

Shreya's expression becomes amused as she arches a teasing brow. "Well, I mean, that's a little fast even for me, but if you insist."

Brielle laughs. "I actually really could use your help. I need backup for a possibly dangerous meeting at Central Park—"

"Dangerous meeting?" Shreya bounces on her heels. "Say no more, I'm so in!"

Brielle is really starting to like this girl. "Okay," she giggles, but sobers her voice. "I should warn you, it might get us both in trouble for going without telling the others. But I just have a feeling we shouldn't involve them. Not yet."

Shreya shrugs. "Well, seeing as I just wandered over here for no other reason than a feeling of my own, I totally get it.

And with my luck on your side, I think we'll be just fine." She smiles, but Brielle notices a flicker of doubt in her mahogany eyes.

Still, Logan had nothing but great things to say about Shreya's luck and hunches during their rescue of Cassandra. Brielle feels a great sense of confidence in the thought of having Shreya as her wing woman, and feeling confident is exactly what she needs right now.

"Great, let's go!" She taps out a quick text to Kerrim to reschedule their plans, then she and Shreya head for the bus that will take them to Central Park.

Shreya is an absolute delight during their bus ride. She tells Brielle all about her life traveling from place to place every time her parents opened up a new resort. She's met so many interesting people and seen so many interesting things. Brielle gets the sense that Shreya's never had a bad day in her life. She can't help but envy that. Shreya was adopted on the first day in the orphanage, and her parents sound like the most amazing, loving people.

Brielle hates herself for feeling jealous, but her own story is far less sunshine and roses. She's had to struggle for every good thing in her life, and often her best intentions have backfired on her. What must it be like to be so gifted like Shreya? It's no wonder the girl is always so bubbly and perky. She has no reason to be any other way. But despite the slight sting of envy, Shreya's joy is contagious. It's almost as if the bad things don't seem quite so bad under Shreya's ray of light.

When they get to the park, the afternoon sun is casting dark shadows under all the trees, making it difficult to make out the many bodies scattered beneath them. Even though Brielle isn't certain, she has a feeling she knows who might be waiting for them at the lake.

She sees the gray hair as soon as they round the bend,

confirming her suspicions, and anger boils inside her chest, causing her hands to clench into fists. She doubles her pace as they approach, practically stomping on still-damp grass as she cuts across the lawn.

"You!" she barks, and Solomon turns around, a charming smile spreading his goatee.

"Ah, Brielle, I wasn't too sure you'd come."

"I shouldn't have," she grinds out, tempted to unleash her penance power on him and crumple him at her feet. Pitch knows he's done plenty of terrible things in his life to leave him crippled for days. "Where's the book?"

He puts up his hands in a calming gesture. "Don't you fret, it's in good, safe hands. I'm sure you'll learn soon enough."

What the pitch is that supposed to mean? "You promised the book to me, then you double crossed me, and now everyone on my team is pissed at me—"

"Except for me," Shreya chimes in behind her.

Solomon clasps his hands behind him and steps forward. "Well, it's not actually the book you need but the information inside it. Namely, the location of the Staff, which I did manage to glean before I forfeited the book to its new owner. I'm willing to hand over the location to you, no questions asked."

Brielle glowers at him for a long moment, debating whether to let him speak or just punch him in the face. "And then what, I find it and you steal that from me, too?"

One of his caterpillar eyebrows arches wryly. "If I were going to steal the Staff, why would I tell you where to find it rather than retrieving it myself?"

She opens her mouth to retort, but the statement has her stumped. The logic there is pretty sound, and she doesn't sense a hint of deceit in him. Though, she didn't with their earlier arrangement either. Could it be that he decided after the fact to give the book to someone else? Although that means Solomon's loyalties never remain in one place, all the more reason not to trust him.

But she doesn't have to trust him to hear him out. If they get the location of the Staff, she doesn't need to have any further contact with him. He never has to know it's actually in their possession.

She crosses her arms obstinately. "Fine, tell me where to find it."

He reaches inside his blazer and pulls out a folded slip of paper, offering it to her. Brielle eyes him warily before accepting it. She unfolds it and skims it over, feeling Shreya lean in to have a read too. It's a list of latitudes and longitudes rather than a single address.

She waves it in the air. "What am I supposed to do with this?" She knows her voice is catty, but she's had enough of Solomon's treachery, and politeness has gone completely out the window.

"The Staff is in two pieces," he explains. "Each of those coordinates points to one of the pieces. They can only be joined with this." He opens his other hand to reveal a purple amulet with the Gemini symbol woven over it in shiny black metal.

She reaches for it, but Solomon pulls it back. "Once you have all of the pieces in your possession, call me and I will show you how to bind them with the amulet."

Her teeth grind with the clenching of her jaw. She knew he was going to weasel his way into this somehow. "Why not just give me the amulet and tell me how to bind them?"

"Because I want to make sure the Staff is in safe hands before it can be used as the powerful weapon it is," he says. Again, no alarms in her lie detection. Though, with Solomon, that isn't saying much.

What choice does Brielle have but to go along with this?

She really has no knowledge of this Staff or what it does, and certainly not how to bind it with this mysterious amulet. But she'll be damned if she's going to fall for another one of his traps.

"Fine," she says finally. "We'll find the pieces of the staff, and we may or may not call you when we do. But answer me one thing. How do you know so much about the Staff?"

"I knew the man who hid it," he confides. "Alden, the soldier sent by the Gemini King to protect the heirs. He brought the Staff with him, desperate to keep it out of Chardis's clutches. I held it my hands once, and I know for a fact that it can never fall into Chardis's hands. Knowing it was too dangerous to keep intact, he separated the pieces and hid them in various locations around New York City. He only ever wrote of their locations in that book."

Brielle is surprised by this. Solomon knew Alden? Her heart warms at the thought of the man who'd been her silent protector all her life, watching over from the shadows.

She wants to ask in what capacity they knew each other, but Solomon stiffens and says, "I must take my leave, ladies. I'll be expecting your call." Then he shoves his hands in his pockets and strolls along the sidewalk to the park's entrance, taking the amulet with him.

Brielle exchanges a glance with Shreya.

"So what now?" Shreya asks. "We gonna go find these pieces?"

Brielle lets out a sigh. "I think we have to."

"Then what are we waiting for?" Shreya skips ahead back in the direction they came, ever the eager beaver.

Brielle knows one thing as they embark on this next adventure. She's not going to give Solomon the benefit of the doubt this time. She's going to make absolutely certain he can't double cross them again.

She has a plan of her own.

FRANK

Frank holds tightly onto Bea's hand as they enter the little diner tucked between a felafel house and a Taco Bell. The place is empty, and he wonders if it's the food or the décor. The interior is outfitted in green and what was once white, but is now an aged cream.

But neither Frank nor Bea are here to eat or enjoy the faded Christmas ambiance. They're here to see the only person in the diner. The woman tucked in the furthest booth from the door.

They exchange a glance. The knowledge they're doing something good, something so much bigger than themselves, passes between them. Bea squeezes Frank's hand and he returns the gesture, warmth filling his chest.

How he loves this woman. He'd be nothing without her. When they first learned they couldn't have children, they'd been devastated. The prospect of just the two of them had felt hollow. But then they'd discovered that purpose could fill that void. That they can make a difference in ways they'd never imagined.

Learning aliens exist had changed everything.

And then that knowledge brought Brielle into their life.

"For Brielle," Bea murmurs.

"For our family," Frank agrees.

They slip into the booth across from the woman wearing a green cashmere sweater, as if she's trying to camouflage herself, even in this deserted, forgotten diner.

"Olivia, wonderful to see you again," Frank says with a smile.

She smiles back. "Frank, you're looking well considering your recent...absence."

"Thank you for your help in getting me out," he says. "Your lawyers were impressive."

Olivia waves her cup of coffee dismissively. "Money well spent considering your loyalty. Even someone as powerful as Richard Sinclair couldn't stop us. Operation Castle may not exist according to most of the population, but we have powerful supporters."

Frank's mouth twists. "Richard Sinclair's evil will catch up with him," he growls. "It's only a matter of time."

Bea rests a warm hand on his forearm. "He'll reap what he's sown."

"And the world will be a better place for it," Olivia says, her lip curling before she takes a sip of her coffee. "We've been following that bastard for a while now, especially since he betrayed you."

Frank's eyebrows contract. "And?"

"He's a slimy one, that's for sure." Olivia puts her mug down and leans forward. "Although we're pretty sure he directly opposes everything Operation Castle stands for."

That has Frank's brows lowering even further. "He thinks extraterrestrials are a threat."

Bea stiffens as if it's a personal attack. "He's met Brielle. How can he consider her a threat?"

"He's greedy and short-sighted," Olivia says, her mouth twisting with distaste. "We need to work with aliens, not against them."

Frank and Bea nod. They came to this conclusion years ago.

"Which is why we have Operation Castle," Olivia adds, adjusting her shoulders so she sits a little straighter. "Collaboration will enable us to harness alien technology and keep Earth safe. Alliances are what will save lives."

Frank nods, determination settling deep in his bones. "Has there been any news?"

Olivia shakes her head. "The wormhole has been quiet. And there's been no sign of the dark entity they call Chardis."

Bea's hand tightens around Frank's. "Then we need to act soon," she says. "Things won't stay quiet for long."

"Yes," he agrees, intensity keeping his voice low. "We need to protect the Zodiacs."

They are the key to forming an alliance with those beyond the borders of Earth. Working together protects them and humanity.

Olivia's eyes sharpen. "It's time to talk to Brielle."

Frank and Bea glance at each other, a frission of nervousness passing between them.

"Frank? Bea?" Olivia asks sharply. "Brielle is our way in with the Zodiacs. It's the reason you adopted her once we identified her as one."

Another glance and they nod mutely. That's how their family started—from the lofty intentions to ally with aliens and protect countless lives. But then Brielle snuck into their hearts. She made their family whole.

They'd both be heartbroken if they lost that.

Bea squeezes Frank's hand, then maintains the pressure. "She'll understand. She's a Zodiac. They're fighting for peace and freedom from evil just as much as we are."

Frank nods. "Maybe you should talk to her," he says. "Your bond with her is a strong one."

"So is yours," she says, love and conviction shining from her eyes. "She's your daughter, too."

Olivia clasps her coffee mug again. "Frank, I'd suggest you retrieve the Staff now that you have the book." Her face hardens. "We don't have much time. Others are searching for it with just as much urgency."

Including the Zodiacs, because they have no idea how dangerous the Staff can be.

They turn back simultaneously to Olivia. "I'll speak to Brielle," says Bea.

"And I'll find the Staff," says Frank.

Olivia smiles, although her face and eyes remain hard. "Excellent. I don't need to remind you what will happen if Operation Castle fails."

One word unwillingly rises in Frank's mind.

War.

21

KERRIM

The smell of the disgusting brown coffee fills the air in the café as Kerrim waits for Brielle to arrive after her shift has ended.

He absentmindedly stirs a straw around a glass of bubbly strawberry soda. Kerrim's not much for the flavor, but he's always preferred the color red. It's the color of his home world. The flora of Araklya are all reds of various shades and hues. The view from his bedchamber at the royal palace is a carpet of red araka trees for miles and miles, and he now misses the sight he often took for granted. He finds the greenery of this planet quite dull, just like the rest of its lifeforms.

His phone on the table in front of him vibrates, calling him back from his fond memories of home, and he swipes the screen open to see a message from Brielle.

"Something came up and I'll have to reschedule. I'll call you later."

The triumphant grin he'd been wearing all day flattens into a frown. He hadn't expected her to cancel. This is a disappointment, but honestly only a slight one. He still managed to cause further friction between Brielle and Tristan. Perhaps this cancellation means he's now freed up to create more rifts amongst the rest of Zodiacs.

Abandoning the unsatisfactory beverage, he slips out of the booth and heads back to Tristan's house. When he arrives, Tristan is in the dining room, deep in conversation with Cassandra, Jareth and Veronica—a heated debate is more like it. He lingers a moment to listen in case he can use this argument later.

"What the pitch were you thinking, Cassandra?" Tristan scolds, his complexion pale with what looks like panic. "How could you do so such a thing? We're not murderers. We're here to protect the people of Earth, not punish them for crimes against us."

Cassandra's eyes are filled with defiant indignation, and Kerrim chuckles at himself for this other little bamboozle he played on them. "Tristan, I swear to you, I have no idea what he's talking about. I did not kill my dad."

"But Veronica and I *saw* you do it, Cassandra," Jareth protests. "At the park just a few hours ago. You said he deserved what he got."

She shakes her head and bites her bottom lip, clearly aggravated. "I wasn't even at the park this morning. I skipped my jog to sleep in."

Jareth scoffs. "I can't believe you're denying this. And it wasn't just us who saw you. A pedestrian was there too, with his dog who had a camera on his collar. Who knows what that poor guy is going to do with that footage. I'm surprised it's not already all over social media."

Cassandra crosses her arms and stalks closer to Jareth, eyes narrowed. "Oh really? Good, let's go find this guy and see this so-called footage. Then I can prove to you I didn't do it."

"Cassandra, I hate to say this, but...is it possible that

maybe you…lost track of time?" Veronica suggests gingerly. "Maybe all the stuff with your dad affected you more than you realize."

Cassandra throws her hands up, exasperated. "No, it's not possible. I. Didn't. Do. It."

"We saw you," Veronica insists, but without the accusation in her tone that Jareth has.

"You know what, fine," Cassandra snaps. "I'll track this old guy and his dog down myself and prove it to all of you. I don't know who you saw at the park, but it damn sure wasn't me."

Tristan closes in on Cassandra until he's mere inches from her and puts his hands on her shoulders. "Until we figure out what really happened, I think it's best if you stay here and let us deal with the footage. If it really wasn't you, then we'll see that in the video. Until then, please don't leave this house."

Cassandra jerks away from Tristan's hold, crosses her arms and rolls her eyes. "Ugh. Whatever." Then she stalks off down the hall toward her room.

Jareth steps forward. "I'm worried about her. She's not acting like herself. The Cassandra we know wouldn't do something so reckless. I think her time under Richard's capture really messed with her head. She's a danger to everyone."

"Wait just a minute," Veronica chimes in. "I'm not advocating what she did, but putting myself in her shoes, I probably would've killed him, too. I mean, he's abused her for years and years, and then he abducts her and drugs and tortures her. Even I wouldn't have been able to just sit back and do nothing. It's not like she can go to the cops and report what he did without outing the rest of us. And, on the bright side, this does eliminate one of our biggest enemies."

Tristan and Jareth gawk at her in outrage.

"You seriously think she did us a favor?" Jareth asks. "Once that video gets out, guess who's going to be the number-one-most-wanted. In all the leaked footage so far, at least the Zodiacs have been portrayed as heroes. Now they'll think we really are the villains the media wants everyone to believe we are."

"But she wasn't in her suit," Veronica argues.

"That doesn't matter," Tristan declares, pinching the bridge of his nose with his thumb and index finger. "It's not like just anyone can go around throwing fireballs at people. The world saw her do the same thing to the asteroid in her suit. It won't take much for them to connect the dots that she's one of us."

"I think Cassandra needs to be benched indefinitely," Jareth suggests. "And maybe get some therapy. We can handle things without her for a while."

Veronica shakes her head. "You can't do that. Cassandra's an integral part of this team. If you exile her, you'll only make her feel more fragile and alone. She needs us to embrace her and support her right now, not exclude her. She just killed her father, for god's sake! Can you even imagine what she might be going through? What she might be feeling right now?"

They both turn to Tristan for his final say. "First, let's deal with the video issue. Then we'll decide what to do about Cassandra."

Veronica sighs. "Alright, well, I've got to go meet my dad. Please don't make any decisions without me. Cassandra needs an advocate." She pulls her messenger bag over her shoulder and heads out the front door, leaving the two guys to whisper to themselves.

Seeing as the trio seem to be wrestling with enough contention already, Kerrim decides to leave them to it and venture for other members to mess with.

As he walks past the living room, he sees Eric napping on one of the couches. Ada isn't with him, which can only mean she's in HQ—or on another solo stealth mission with Brielle, but seeing how upset Eric had been after that stunt for not being included, Kerrim doubts that possibility.

"Eric," he whispers as he approaches the couch.

A snore escapes Eric's throat in response, ensuring Kerrim that he's well and truly deep in sleep. Excellent.

Kerrim calls the shadows as he walks down the hall toward the secret entrance, changing his appearance to Eric's right down to the blue t-shirt and jeans he's wearing.

Time to indulge in a little mayhem.

Just as Kerrim predicted, Ada is indeed typing away at the largest computer, her attention so focused on her work that she doesn't even seem to notice his entrance. Adopting Eric's posture and swagger, Kerrim takes a seat in the swivel chair beside her and sets his features into a scowl.

"Ada, we need to talk," he says, his voice the perfect parrot of Eric's.

Ada startles out of her fixation and turns to him, her brows instantly creasing when she registers the look on his face. "Yeah, what's up?"

He lets out a long-suffering sigh. "I was trying to hold my peace about things, but I just can't do it anymore. When we got back together, you said things would be different. You promised you wouldn't hide anything from me anymore. And yet you just went rogue with Brielle to make a deal with Cadbury behind my back."

"I didn't want to keep that from you, but it wasn't my secret to tell," she argues defensively. "Brielle swore me to secrecy, and I was certain her plan would work."

He lets the volume of his voice rise in forced anger. "That's the problem. You always think you know best, when in fact you don't. You never think to consult me on the most important matters. I'm just expected to go along with whatever you decide, and that's not a partnership."

"But Eric, I—"

He cuts her off. "And don't even get me started on Esther. You spend more time with her than you ever do with me. She's more in a relationship with you than I am. Is this what the rest of our lives are going to be like? You glued to a computer and making executive decisions and leaving me to pick up the pieces by myself?" He shakes his head and throws up his hands. "I need some space. Can that at least be my decision? Can I have some time away from you?"

Before she can answer, he jumps out of the chair and storms out of the room, making it clear with a scowl before he leaves that he doesn't want to be followed.

And she doesn't. The door closes behind him, and it stays that way. He grins impishly.

Two relationships down. Who's next?

He strolls back to the main area of the house, making sure that Eric is still fast asleep. Jareth is in the kitchen by himself, frowning over a bagel that only has cream cheese spread over half of it. Target acquired.

Kerrim changes his appearance to that of Veronica's. He has to get her outfit down to the tee, because unlike Ada, Jareth will absolutely notice any discrepancies in her attire. The two of them are so in love, it's actually quite disgusting.

When Kerrim is certain he has mimicked Veronica exactly, even manifesting the shoulder bag she'd carried out, he hurries into the kitchen as if he'd just come in the front door, pulls off the shoulder bag and sets it on the counter.

Jareth quickly looks up at him, apprehension and curiosity in his dark eyes. "I thought you left to meet your dad?"

"I was going to, but I had to come back. This couldn't wait." Kerrim hates the sound of Veronica's voice in his mouth, but it's a worthwhile nuisance. "I realized that you're right about Cassandra. While I feel bad for her, she really is too much of a threat right now. She's not thinking clearly, and she could put the rest of us—namely you—in danger. She's a wild card, and maybe one that should be left in the deck for a while."

Jareth's eyes widen in surprise. "What made you change your mind?"

It makes Kerrim almost physically ill to play the gushing romantic, but he has to in order to pull this off. He rounds the counter and puts his arms around Jareth's neck. "You did. Worrying about what could happen to you if she flies off the handle again. I couldn't bear it if anything happened to you, because of her or anyone else. And if changing my vote can help keep you safe, then that's what I'm going to do."

He pecks Jareth on the cheek, impatiently looking forward to this charade being over so he can wipe his mouth. Maybe rinse with the mediocre fluoride solution in the bathroom.

"Thanks, babe," Jareth says, love shining in his muddy brown eyes. "I'll speak with Tristan again and let him know. Ultimately, whatever Tristan decides is what we'll do."

"And I'm sure you can help him see reason, just like you did with me." Kerrim smiles with Veronica's lips, then withdraws and slings the bag over his shoulder again. "Okay, I really do have to go. Call you later." He waves Veronica's dainty fingers and jogs toward the front door, opening and closing it to make it sound like he left. Then he returns to his true form and sits on the couch, turning on the TV.

Now to sit back and watch the fruits of his labor ripen and rot as chaos ensues.

22

SHREYA

T he first pair of coordinates takes Shreya and Brielle to a subway in the heart of New York City.

"Are you sure this is the right place?" Shreya asks as they stand before the stairway at the corner of 5th and Main where people continuously file up and down like racks of meat on a conveyor belt.

"This is where the coordinates lead," Brielle says, looking back and forth from her phone to the stairway, dubiously chewing her bottom lip. "Not right here, exactly, but somewhere down there."

Shreya shrugs. "Well, alright then. Let's go explore. I've never actually ridden the subway before." She leads the way down the steps, oddly enjoying the mingling smells of the Big Apple's underbelly—a strange cocktail of cigarette smoke, body odor, stale liquor and perfume.

"I don't think you'll get to just yet," Brielle says as she hurries behind her. "According to Esther's GPS map, the exact location is halfway between here and the next stop. We'll have to walk there on foot."

Shreya stops on the platform amidst the bustling pedestrians and tosses back a quizzical look. Brielle just nods, and Shreya frowns. "No wonder nobody's found it before."

Brielle takes the lead and heads to the back corner of the platform, looking over her shoulder to make sure no one has noticed them. Shreya snickers through her nose. These people are so preoccupied with themselves, she doubts if they'd notice the pair of them even if they had bombs strapped to their chests.

Satisfied with their anonymity, Brielle slips over the edge down onto the dark track, then holds out a hand to help Shreya down. Shreya doesn't need the assistance, but she obliges Brielle and takes her hand anyway, knowing that she thrives on being able to help others. It's her MO, and who is Shreya to deny her that small joy?

Once they're both down on the track, and after taking another quick glance over their shoulders, they creep into the narrow mouth of the tunnel, darkness swallowing them with each step they take forward. It's not long before all light from the platform behind them is completely snuffed out, and Brielle turns on the flashlight on her phone to guide them.

The beam of light accentuates articles left behind by homeless people—empty beer cans, discarded bottles wrapped in paper bags, cigarette butts. Even a—is that a pair of dirty boxers?

Gross. Shreya scrunches up her nose, but even that admittedly disgusting sight can't suck her excitement out of this venture. She loves every appalling second of it!

They wander for several more minutes, combing every inch of the tunnel with their flashlights and eyes, and Shreya trips over a makeshift walking stick in her search, only narrowly keeping herself afoot.

Brielle turns back. "What was that? Are you okay?" She

seems much more apprehensive and on guard to be here than Shreya is, her body wound tight like a closed spring.

"Fine, just tripped. No biggie." As Shreya casts her glance aside, her flashlight beam catches on something unusual. "That doesn't look like it belongs here."

Brielle rushes over to inspect the spot on the wall Shreya's beam is focused on, then brushes her hand over the Zodiac wheel symbol that looks like it was scribbled with white paint marker. It's crude and imperfect, blending in with all the other graffiti that covers the tunnel walls and ceiling. Nobody would pay it any mind if they weren't actively looking for it.

Brielle brings up her phone screen, the illumination momentarily blinding both of them as they look down at it. After their eyes adjust, they can see that the dot marking their location on the map is right on top of the ping for the coordinates.

"It's right here," Brielle says, running her hands over the symbol once more. "Somewhere. But how do we get to it?"

Shreya steps up to the wall, presses her ear to it and knocks her knuckles in several places. "Right here," she says, pressing her fingertip to the spot. "It's hollow."

"And look, there's a seam," Brielle gasps, pointing to a long line so narrow and covered in dirt that, again, no one would see it if they weren't looking for it. They both follow the line with their fingertips to find that it's actually a long rectangle.

Brielle's fingers press on the edges and corners of the seam, trying to gain purchase underneath, but the gap is far too narrow and nothing seems to budge.

"How the heck do we get it open?" Brielle asks, frowning in frustration.

An idea comes to Shreya, and just like with finding the

Nebula HQ a few days ago, she *feels* like it's important, like it's what she's supposed to do. So she goes with it. She gently pushes in front of Brielle, getting down on her knees, and places both hands right on top of the Zodiac symbol. Then, with every ounce of strength she can muster—which isn't saying much with her small size—she gives it a forceful shove.

With a puff of dust all around the edges that makes them both cough and wave in front of their faces, the section of wall gives in, then slides slowly to the left, revealing a narrow compartment behind it. There, collecting spider webs and all manner of industrial filth, sits a long rod, somehow still managing to shine with metallic grace.

They stare at it for a long moment, neither one daring to reach in lest the compartment slide closed and trap their hand.

But Shreya, unable to contain herself for long, throws caution to the wind and snatches the object as fast as she can. No explosions detonate, no alarms go off. The compartment simply closes slowly shut again, as if somehow knowing the right people claimed its bounty and its job is done.

"Whoa," Brielle says, gawking at it with awe. "It's beautiful."

"So, this is the weapon that can defeat Chardis," Shreya breathes, almost cradling the rod in her palms.

"Only half of it," Brielle corrects. "The other half is waiting for us at the next set of coordinates."

Shreya nods. "Right. Well, let's go get it!" She pops to her feet, just as a flash of light fills the tunnel from around the bend.

"Shreya!" Brielle shouts, then grabs her by the arm and not-so-gently presses her against the wall, trapping her between it and herself just in time for the large train to speed past.

They stand like that, frozen in place, neither one moving

even to breathe, afraid that the slightest motion will push them into the whizzing side of the train and turn them into Zodiac confetti. For a few minutes after, they remain, and Shreya's sure she can feel Brielle's heart beating the same frantic tune as her own.

"I think we're okay now," Shreya says, patting Brielle's stiff back.

Brielle lets out the breath she'd been holding and steps back with shaky legs. "That was *so* close."

Suddenly, Shreya throws her arms around Brielle's neck and hugs her tightly. "You saved me."

Brielle's blushing when Shreya withdraws. "Of course. I'm just glad I was quick enough."

Shreya's heart warms her chest and all the way over her face. She's glad that Brielle is so eager to help, to save others, because without that virtue, Shreya would've been a pixie pancake.

23

BRIELLE

B rielle's still shaky as they make their way up the stairs. She thought Shreya was supposed to be lucky, but she narrowly became roadkill down there. Maybe her luck was that the right people were always there at the right time? Either way, it did seem to be her luck that both found where the Staff was hiding and figured out how to get to it.

"Where's the next location?" Shreya asks as they land on the sidewalk above ground. She, on the other hand, doesn't seem the least bit shaken by her near-death experience. Brielle almost envies her ability to be constantly positive no matter what happens.

"Um…" Brielle holds up her phone. "Esther, can you ping us the location of the next coordinates?"

"Of course. The location is now pinned on your map," Esther replies.

Brielle swipes the screen open, and finding the pin on the map, she stops short. "Uh, Esther, are you sure this is correct?"

"Assuming the satellite I accessed is on the proper trajectory, that location should be one hundred percent accurate," Esther says.

Brielle just stares down at the screen, realizing that her head is shaking subtly from side to side.

"What's wrong?" Shreya asks, leaning closer to look at the screen over Brielle's shoulder. "Is it somewhere bad? More dangerous than the subway tunnel?"

"No," Brielle says softly, still staring at the pin. "It's just… that's the orphanage where I spent most of my life."

"Whoa. Seriously?" Shreya blows up at one of her pixie cut bangs that's fallen in front of her eyes, but it falls back down so she swipes it away with an irritated hand.

"And it burned down a few weeks ago," Brielle adds. "The other part of the Staff might not even be there anymore." A lump forms at the base of her neck.

"Only one way to find out." Shreya smiles and waggles her brows eagerly, then walks to the curb, puts her index finger and thumb in her mouth and whistles loudly for an upcoming taxi. It pulls up a few feet ahead of them, and she waves Brielle over as she catches up to it. "I always wanted to do that," she says with a flare of mischief as she opens the back door for Brielle.

Shreya fidgets and bounces happily on the way there, but Brielle can't match her enthusiasm. She hasn't been to the orphanage since the fire. Flashes of that night crack and pop in her mind like the blazing wooden beams that almost killed everyone—that *did* kill Sister Agatha. That had been the last place Brielle had wanted to go for weeks. She'd even gone out of her way to avoid passing it while riding her bike around town.

But now she had no choice but to return. If the other half of the Staff is even still there.

Would it have survived the fire? If it had, could one of the firefighters or paramedics have found it amongst the rubble and taken it with them? Or perhaps one of the nuns in the clean-up crew picked it up and now has it stored in a box somewhere at the temporary housing facility. Maybe she should check with them first.

A denial to that thought stops it from finishing forming in her mind. No. She can't avoid the place, or the memories it brings with it, forever. Especially not now.

In forty-five minutes, the taxi pulls up in front of the construction site that was once Brielle's childhood home. The church had paid for the reconstruction to begin, but it seemed to be a slow process. There was nothing here but a wooden framework of the new plan, and stacks of cement blocks and bricks off to the side. Luckily there weren't any workers in attendance at this moment, but still, Brielle doesn't like their odds of actually finding anything.

"That'll be sixty-five fifty," the cabby calls from the front seat as Brielle reluctantly opens the door to get out. His New York accent is so sharp, it would have been comical if the situation weren't so somber. "Extra because you had me take you outta the city. You shoulda mentioned that part."

Shreya slaps him a few bills. "Here you go. Thanks!"

"Yeah, have a nice day," he replies like he doesn't actually care if they do or not and counts the cash. Then he drives off, and they are left alone to stare at the bones of the new church.

Neither of them says anything as they crunch over the dead grass toward the structure. Shreya is scanning the ground everywhere she walks, looking for clues, but Brielle finds it hard to focus on the task at hand. Her heart is in her throat the entire time, pounding with each heavy step she takes, and it's all she can do not to let the tears pour out.

She imagines children frolicking past, hears echoes of the laughter they used to share as they played. She sees the remains of the rose hedges she'd tended with such care for years, and every tender memory of Sister Agatha they'd ever made here together replays in her mind.

On autopilot, she steps through the framework and onto the cement foundation, which seems to be the only part of this near and dear place that survived the fire. She walks through what used to be the kitchens, where she'd spent most of her adolescent life helping the nuns. She discovered her love of cooking here. And Sister Agatha had helped her foster it.

Finally, sorrow overcomes her, and she can't keep the tears at bay any longer. They flood out as if breaking through a dam, and she crumples to her knees, covering her face with her hands.

"Brielle?" she hears Shreya ask a few feet away. Her feet crunch over grass and slap on the cement as she runs over, and soon Brielle can feel Shreya's hands on her shoulders. "I'm sorry. I didn't realize—I… You must have had a lot of memories about this place."

Brielle nods and hiccups on a cry. "Sister Agatha died in that fire," she sobs. "She was like a mother to me." She lifts her head out of her hands to look blurrily at Shreya. "I miss her so much!"

Shreya pulls her in for a comforting hug, letting Brielle cry all over her rock band t-shirt as she rubs her back. "I'm so sorry." The eternal optimism and chipper pitch are absent from her voice, replaced by a soft acceptance. "Despite knowing that aliens and superpowers exist, I still believe there's a higher power out there somewhere behind it all. Sister Agatha surely believed that, too. I'm sure she's in a better place now. And I'm sure she's looking down on you, proud of the kick-ass heroin that you are."

Shreya's words make Brielle's heart blossom with both love and pain. And hope. Sister Agatha devoted her life to her belief in God, in life after death. And if there is a Heaven, there's not a single shred of doubt in Brielle's mind that Sister Agatha is there, probably chiding a child spirit not to pick his nose.

The thought makes her laugh, and Shreya pulls away from Brielle. "You okay now?"

Brielle nods and sniffles. "I think so."

Shreya smiles and looks down, and her lips go from spread to rounded as her eyes widen. "You've got to be kidding me."

"What?" Brielle follows Shreya's face downward, then, stunned, scuttles backward to reveal the concrete beneath them.

There, on the very spot on which Brielle had collapsed, another Zodiac wheel is carved into a stone slab with expert precision.

Of course! The foundation was the only thing that wouldn't burn, that would withstand the tests of time! Clever Alden.

"The staff must be under it!" Shreya chirps. "But how do we get it up? That sucker looks like it's really in there."

Brielle snaps her head up and looks all around. A set of yard tools rests on one of the brick piles, including four shovels. Without a word, she springs to her feet and runs to grab two of them. Rushing back to the spot, she hands Shreya one of the shovels, then wedges the tip of her own into one of the corners of the slab. Shreya follows suit, and together the two of them pry at the slab with all their might.

The mortar around the slab begins to crumble little by little, and after a good thirty minutes of wrenching, the slab finally tips. They fall to their knees and dig their fingers around the edges, then tug on the slab so hard Brielle's arms feel like they're going to pop out of their sockets. The slab budges only a few inches. They catch their breath and try again.

After three more attempts, they finally have the slab moved enough that they can reach into the hidden compartment it sat atop. Something shiny winks at them in spotty sunlight that spills through the gaps in the clouds overhead.

This time, Brielle doesn't hesitate to reach in and grab it, not caring what sort of creepy crawlies might be down there. She closes her hand around the object and pulls it out to see an intricately woven metal piece that must be the head of the Staff. It's breathtaking! There's an empty slot at its center where it looks like a jewel or something should go. Brielle realizes that must be where the amulet that Solomon has belongs.

That means she has to call him now.

Getting to her feet, she dials Solomon's number and waits for him to answer. "I have it."

"Excellent! Where are you?"

"Grace Orphanage," she replies soberly.

Solomon chuckles. "Clever Alden." She hates that he said the same thing she'd just recently thought. "I'll be right there."

He hangs up, and Brielle and Shreya wait.

Brielle's heart pounds in her chest as the minutes tick by. She doesn't trust Solomon. He might turn up with a handful of Skins for all she knows. Though he wasn't lying when he said he changed sides, that doesn't mean he hadn't recently changed his allegiances again. Whatever the case, she won't be double-crossed again.

This time, she has a backup plan. She just hopes she doesn't want to use it.

His blue sedan pulls up and he jogs across the brown lawn toward them. "Where are the pieces?" he asks.

Brielle holds up the head, and Shreya pulls the rod out from behind her back where she'd been keeping it under the shirt tucked into her jeans. Solomon's eyes light up as he takes in the two pieces. He approaches, pulling the purple amulet out of his inside blazer pocket, then extends his free hand, silently requesting the ancient artifacts.

Shreya glances at Brielle cautiously, and Brielle nods, handing over her the head, so Shreya relinquishes the rod. Solomon takes both, holding them together where they join. "You see, without the amulet, the two pieces won't stay together. But with it…" He brings the amulet closer, and like a super magnet, it's sucked from his hand and into the empty bevel where the head and rod meet.

The entire staff glows faintly for a moment, the purple gem in the amulet flashing with light, and it feels as though a faint shock wave reverberates from the now intact weapon.

"Thank you, Solomon," Brielle says, stepping closer and extending a hand. "We'll make sure it gets put in a safe place."

He steps backward, chuckling softly. "Now, darlin', I can't just hand it over to you. This is the most dangerous weapon in the entire universe." His face becomes serious, determined, as he looks at it. "And it must be destroyed."

Brielle's eyes narrow. Solomon didn't disappoint her expectations. "You can't do that. It's the only thing that can defeat Chardis."

"I don't personally believe that," he says, turning to walk away. "But it would destroy everything if it fell into his hands. I refuse to let that happen."

No. Not this time. Brielle reaches into her back pocket and pulls out the zip lock bag she'd been saving for just this eventuality. Ripping it open, she removes the chloroform-soaked rag, runs up behind Solomon, and clasps it over his mouth.

He struggles, clawing at her hands and trying to buck her off of him. But each labored breath he inhales only makes the chloroform work faster, and soon the two of them topple over onto the ground.

"Holy cow, I can't believe you just did that!" Shreya shrieks. "That was insane! What did you do to him?"

Brielle wrests her arms from around Solomon's neck and gets up, dusting herself off. "Chloroform. I didn't want to hurt him, but I wasn't about to let him take that Staff." She reaches underneath his unconscious body and wrenches the Staff out from under him. "We'll make sure he never gets his hands on it again."

Staff proudly in hand, they walk away from the reviving orphanage, leaving Solomon where he lays, face down. Man, is he going to be pissed when he wakes up.

24

CASSANDRA

Cassandra's angry footsteps echo off the walls as she stomps up the stairs to her new room at Tristan's house. She can't believe the bullshit Jareth and Veronica were saying. Accusing her of being stupid enough to attack her father in broad daylight, in a public park no less? And then grounding her like she's a petulant child.

What do they have against her all of a sudden? She had kinda liked Jareth before all this, and Veronica with her refreshingly give-no-shits attitude. She just can't understand why they would lie about something this outrageous.

She storms into her room and slams the door, plopping down on the bed. And a realization hits her.

Is her father really dead? They said they saw her blast him with a fireball. Sure, she'd been tempted to do that very thing since she escaped his capture, been fantasizing how and when she would do it. But she didn't leave the house today. Her alarm had gone off and she'd silenced it. This had been the first time, pretty much ever, that she'd skipped a run. But she very much needed some mental rest.

She's not completely convinced that the effects of the drug they slipped her have worn off. She hasn't actually seen anything that wasn't there, but the nightmares that have plagued her the past few nights have been hellish.

Jareth claimed that a pedestrian had seen her do it, too, that he had a video recording the whole thing.

A terrifying thought whispers into her mind, making her heart slam against her rib cage with an audible *thud* that rings in her ears.

What if she really did do it? What if she'd somehow sleep-walked to the park and acted out the darkest, most secret desire of her vengeful heart? Or maybe she hadn't actually ever gone back to sleep at all. Maybe she had gone for her run after all, killed him, and then somehow blacked out the whole thing.

Omigod.

Her hands begin to tremble where they rest in her lap, and that same cold that had chilled her to the bone when she'd been tied up in the basement bites at her fingertips, subduing her inner flame. She swallows down the fearful bile that's begun to climb up her throat.

If there really is a video of her killing her dad, she needs to see it, before anyone else does. She needs to prove to herself that she's not losing her mind. How can she convince anyone else of her innocence if she's not convinced herself?

Damn Tristan's order for her stay put and let them handle it. She's going to get that video feed before they do.

But how? She doesn't even know what this pedestrian looks like, let alone how to even go about finding him.

She looks down at her shaking fingers and clenches them in frustration, then notices the watch on her wrist.

"Esther?" she asks.

"Yes, Cassandra?" Esther's neutral voice replies.

Cassandra's not even sure what to ask. "Um, can you possibly help me locate someone in the neighborhood?"

"Who would you like to locate?" Esther asks.

"That's the thing." Cassandra sucks her bottom lip between her teeth. "I don't exactly know. He would be an older man with a dog, who possibly frequently walks the dog around the park on Cherry Avenue."

"I will start by pulling up the local property records of every man between the ages of forty-five and eighty who owns or rents a domicile in the neighborhood," Esther says. "I've compiled a list of twenty-five people. Now cross-referencing that list with everyone who has a dog licensed with the county. That shortens the list to three. Of those three, there is one man recently recorded by the streetlight cameras at the corner of Cherry Avenue and Third Street walking a German Shepherd. Here is the address on record."

Her watch dings, and an address pops up on the little screen. One-sixty-three Crest Hill Road. That's only a few blocks from here!

"Thank you, Esther," Cassandra says, quickly pulling on and tying her tennis shoes. Looks like she'll be going for that run after all.

"You're welcome, Cassandra."

She stands and heads for the door, then stops. Tristan told her she can't leave. They'll stop her if she tries to go out the front door. That leaves her with only one option. Great.

Moving to the window, she slowly lifts it open, hoping no one downstairs can hear the subtle *creak* of metal sliding on metal. She peers down the wall, debating just how she's going to get down. It's too far of a drop to just jump.

A branch looms in her peripheral vision, and Cassandra turns to her right to assess the distance. It's possibly about three feet away from the window. Can she jump that far?

She climbs onto the windowsill, hooking the treads of her shoes into the groove. *Please don't miss.* She takes a moment to brace herself, then kicks away from the window with all the strength of her track muscles, shooting her arms out desperately toward the branch.

For an impossibly long second, there's nothing but air beneath her, and she's certain she's going to fall.

But her hands scrape along the jagged bark of the branch, her momentum causing her to slip several inches down the length of it. Pain bites into her palms and fingertips. But she's used to it. After years of clenching her fists tight enough to restrain her fire, the crescent scars that mar her palms act as a sort of callous.

Once she's cemented her grip, she swings her legs around the branch and slowly shimmies her way down the tree, planting her feet on solid ground.

She looks up at the window she just left, making sure no one came looking for her. When no head pops out, she sprints in the direction of the address on her watch's screen, taking the back alley in hopes of beating Tristan and Jareth there. She'll be damned if they get the video before she does. This kitty isn't going down without a fight. Not ever again.

It only takes her five minutes to run to Mr. James Anthony's house. The home is small, only one story, and appears to be a bachelor pad as there are no kid toys or traces of a feminine touch in the yard. But how exactly is she going to go about getting inside? Is she really going to break in? Sneak in through a window like the one she just jumped out of? He might have an alarm system.

Does she have any better options, though? She can't just knock on the front door. If she really did do what Jareth and Veronica say, he'll freak out if he sees her.

But then again, if she really did kill her dad, it's not like breaking and entering would be the worst thing she's done today.

Screw it.

She creeps up to the nearest window and attempts to lift it. It pulls up easily, and no beeps sound. But if there was a security system in place, she probably wouldn't hear anything, with how sophisticated those things are these days. That means she needs to be quick.

Cassandra hops onto the ledge and pulls herself inside. She lands in a small living room. Oh yeah, this guy is definitely single. There's nothing in here but a Lazy Boy recliner and Ikea furniture. And a dog. Ah crap.

The German Shepherd perks its head up from the cot it's laying on and looks at her.

"Shh, good boy," she whispers calmingly.

Thankfully, the dog doesn't seem to find her very interesting and tucks its head back into its paws to continue its nap. A breath of relief escapes her, and she makes quick work of scanning the room for any signs of the dog collar camera Jareth mentioned. But there's nothing like that on any of the surfaces, and she's certain it wouldn't still be around the dog's neck.

She moves about the space on tiptoes, hoping the guy isn't still home. What does someone do after they see a girl throw a fireball and kill a man? Call the cops? Call the newspaper? What are the chances he forgot about the camera?

"What the—"

She hears the exclamation before she sees a figure emerge from the hallway to her left, and when she looks in his direction, his face pales to the color of a sheet of paper.

"It's you!" he gasps.

To her utter surprise and horror, the man looking back at her is none other than her father. The man she supposedly killed.

Flashes of the torture he inflicted on her in the basement blaze in her mind, and before she knows what she's doing, she's raised her hands to defend herself, and a powerful heat erupts from her elevated palms, hitting him square in the chest.

His body crumples to the floor, and the dog begins to bark.

Her chest heaves rapidly up and down as she tries to process what just happened. She knew she didn't kill her father. At least, she hadn't earlier. How could she have killed him if he was lying before her, here and now?

His body doesn't budge, nothing but the smoke of his burnt shirt moving in his vicinity. She hedges closer, wanting simultaneously to check if he's really dead and to bolt before he can hurt her again.

"Cassandra?"

She looks up to see Tristan and Jareth rushing in through the hall from where her dad came. Tristan gasps as he looks down at the smoldering body.

"What have you done?"

"Me? What were you guys doing with my dad? Is this some kind of screwed up joke?" she yells, rage warming her palms once more.

"What are you talking about?" Jareth's face is full of blame as he regards her.

Cassandra opens her mouth to accuse them further, but a glimpse at the face of the man on the floor makes her freeze.

This man isn't her dad. He's someone else completely. Someone she's certain she's never seen in her life. And she just killed him. What the heck is happening?

A raspy breath escapes the man's slacked jaw.

"He's still breathing," Tristan exclaims, dropping to his knees at the man's side. "Here, help me with him. We'll get him to a hospital." He glances at Jareth. "And find the doggy cam. We need to destroy it."

Cassandra stands there like a statue, panic and confusion sizzling through her every nerve fiber as she watches them carry the man away.

Maybe she really is losing her mind. What has she done?

BRIELLE

Brielle's pulse gallops in her chest as she and Shreya rush to Tristan's house with the Staff.

As soon as they'd left, she'd wrapped it with her jacket. It wasn't easy to conceal a four-foot-long alien artifact, but she did her best. Rather than risking transporting it on the bus, where Skins could be lurking and ready to steal their hard-won prize, she'd called an Uber instead.

Now they sit in the back seat of the inconspicuous blue Saturn sedan with the Staff gripped firmly over their laps. Luckily, the driver hadn't asked about the strange object wrapped in her jacket, and she'd made certain to inspect his eyes for a silver ring before getting in.

Solomon's going to be furious when he wakes, and she knows they'll all have to face his wrath soon enough. But that doesn't matter. Nothing else matters but getting this price-less weapon back to HQ and safeguarding it from everyone and anyone who might try to take it.

"That was incredible!" Shreya whispers, jiggling her knees slightly so that the Staff bounces with it. "Why don't you look excited? We totally kicked ass back there."

Brielle looks up at the rearview mirror to make sure the driver isn't paying them any attention. "I'm just worried about the ramifications of this."

"What ramifications? That Solomon dude? Who cares if he gets mad."

Brielle frowns. Her betrayal of Solomon isn't what has her heart racing and threatening to burst out of her chest. "It's not just that. How are we going to explain this to Tristan?" He just scolded her for going behind their backs to get to the book, and now she's done it again with the Staff. Is it going to matter that she succeeded this time? Will he be pleased with her?

Shreya makes a face and shakes her head. "Explain what? That we got the Staff? We just found the ultimate weapon in this war. Boom. You're welcome."

Brielle laughs at Shreya's over-simplification, but her chest feels hollow.

"I don't think he's going to see it that way," Brielle says with a sigh, looking down at the wrapped object in her lap. "I think he'll be upset that I went solo again without consulting everyone first. Without telling him. And that I trusted Solomon a second time."

Shreya scoffs. "You're selling yourself way too short. You're a frickin' rock star! If you'd told everyone, they would've gotten in the way. And you didn't trust Solomon. You knew he was gonna do something shady, and the way you chloroformed him, that was badass!"

The driver's eyes flick up at them in the rearview mirror, and Brielle shushes Shreya.

Shreya grimaces and lowers her voice. "All I'm saying is you're not giving yourself enough credit. If the others are upset with how you got this, then so be it." She gives Brielle a knowing look. "But it's not them you're worried about. It's just Tristan. Why do you care so much about what he thinks?"

Brielle doesn't answer, and luckily she doesn't have to.

"Here we are, ladies," says the twenty-something male driver as they pull up at Tristan's driveway. "If you wouldn't mind, I'd love a five-star review."

"Sure thing, will do," Brielle says brusquely as she hastens out of the car. They need to get their precious cargo inside before anyone else might see it, and before the driver can ask any questions.

Hugging the Staff firmly against her chest, she and Shreya run up to the front door. What she sees when she gets inside is not something she ever expected.

The Zodiacs are arguing left and right. Cassandra, Veronica and Jareth are screaming at each other in a tight little circle in the kitchen, and Ada and Eric are squabbling between themselves in the living room. Tristan is doing his best to mediate the kitchen situation, but no one seems to hear him. And Kerrim is just sitting on the couch, watching all this with an almost morbid fascination. Behind the blatant confusion at what's going on, Brielle can't help but feel slightly embarrassed for Kerrim. He just joined them, and he's going to think they're a bunch of petulant teenagers who don't know what they're doing.

He may be right, actually.

She hands the Staff to Shreya, nodding for her to take it to HQ, then heads into the kitchen.

"Hey, what's going on?" she asks.

Everyone starts shouting at once, and Brielle can't make out anything. Jareth accuses Cassandra of being a danger to everyone, and she shoves him, causing Tristan to step in the middle. Cassandra's hands begin to glow menacingly, and Brielle knows she has to stop this before it escalates into something they can't come back from.

"Guys, stop!" Brielle demands, exuding an authority she

didn't know she had. "One person at a time, tell me what this is all about."

"Cassandra ki—" Jareth begins, but Cassandra cuts him off with a "Who said you get to go first?"

Brielle approaches Cassandra and puts her hands on Cassandra's wrists, giving her a firm but calming look. "Cassandra. Please. It's okay. Just calm down." Then she turns to Jareth. "Go ahead, Jareth."

Jareth takes a breath. "Cassandra killed her father earlier today. In broad daylight."

Brielle's eyes and mouth fall into perfect O's. She has no words. She's too stunned to even form an opinion.

"And she was seen by a man who was walking his dog with a video camera strapped to its chest," he explains further. "Then, after we decided she was going to stay here and let us handle it—"

"You decided, you mean," Cassandra butts in, but Jareth ignores her.

"—she accosted the poor guy and almost killed him, too! I think we need to vote right now to keep her benched from any further action. Maybe even take her stone until—"

"No, you can't do that!" Veronica demands. "You'd basically be telling her she's not a Zodiac anymore. And you can't take away her only way of protecting herself."

"Thank you," Cassandra scoffs, flipping her hair over her shoulder.

"You're welcome," Veronica says.

"She doesn't need her suit to protect herself," Jareth argues. "She was dangerous even before she had her stone." He shakes his head in confusion at Veronica. "And I don't understand what's going on with you. You told me earlier that you agreed with me."

"I did no such thing," Veronica snaps, outraged. "I told you, plain as day before I left to see my dad, that I was not okay with this and for you guys not to make any rash decisions without me, without everyone."

"Yes, but then you came back and told me you changed your mind," Jareth says, more confusion infused into his voice.

"No, I most certainly did not," Veronica says, crossing her arms in defiance. "I would never support a woman not having a voice."

"Thank you," Cassandra says again, and Veronica again says, "You're welcome."

Jareth rakes his hands through his black hair. "I can't believe this is happening. Have you all gone insane?"

"Okay, here's what we're going to do," Brielle prefaces, trying not to get overwhelmed. "Each of you will tell your side one at a time. We have to figure out what's got everyone so heated and resolve this. Cassandra, can you explain things as you remember them?"

Cassandra flashes Jareth a triumphant glare at being allowed to go first, then begins. "My alarm went off this morning for me to go for my usual jog around the park, but I dismissed it and decided to sleep in instead. I never was anywhere near the alleged murder, so there's no way I could have been the one to kill the evil bastard."

Jareth opens his mouth to counter, but Brielle stops him by putting a hand up. She doesn't sense any lie in Cassandra's words, and that fills her with the greatest relief. She remembers how bloodthirsty Cassandra was after her rescue, and honestly, she really could imagine Cassandra flying off the handle, though not necessarily in public. The Cassandra she knows is much more calculating than that.

"She's not lying," Brielle says to the others.

"But we saw her do it," Jareth argues. "And so did the old man she almost killed, too, by the way."

"That was different," Cassandra snaps. "I had to prove to

you all that I didn't do it. I wasn't just going to sit back and let you fabricate some video to incriminate me. I wanted to find him for myself, see this so-called video for myself. So I used Esther to track the guy down."

"Okay, then what happened?" Brielle asks, putting her hands up when Jareth tries to interrupt. It's Cassandra's turn to tell her side of the whole thing.

Cassandra takes a deep breath, looking off to the side, and Brielle notices that it's odd how jittery her eye movements seem to be. This isn't the cool and collected Cassandra she's always known. This girl is…fractured. Like a cracked reflection of her former self that might fall apart if you tap on her surface too hard.

"What is it?" Brielle encourages, hoping to convey with her tone that she's supportive and not judgmental.

"The man's face turned into my father's," Cassandra says softly, her head shaking back and forth just a little, as if denying that statement to herself. With a sudden rage, her eyes spear at Jareth. "You *made* me see him! You wanted me out of the way, so you made me see the one thing that would make me hurt an innocent person!" Her voice cracks at the end, and she hiccups on a sob.

Everyone in the room is stunned into silence at her accusation. Even Ada and Eric have stopped bickering and turned their attention this way.

The wind that had seemed to be filling the sails of Jareth's argument stagnate. "You really think I would do something like that?" He looks truly hurt.

"How else do you explain what happened?" Cassandra quips, looking like a lioness in a cage, ready to strike. "You happened to come in right when he turned. You have the ability to make illusions, and you wanted me sidelined so you used your power against me."

His brows raise defensively. "Cassandra, I swear I didn't

do that. I would never do that. I have no issues with you, I promise. I love you as much as I love Tristan and Brielle, and all the other Zodiacs. You're part of our team. I only wanted to get you help before you hurt anyone, or yourself."

Cassandra stares at him with scrutiny for a long time, then she turns to Brielle expectantly.

"He's not lying either," Brielle says. "Whatever you saw with the man, it wasn't Jareth who made you see it."

Tristan sucks in a long breath through his teeth. "Okay, so Cassandra didn't kill Richard, but she did attack the old man because she thought he was Richard. And Jareth didn't make her see whatever she saw. So where does that leave us?"

"I don't know," Brielle says, chewing her lips. "But something here doesn't add up."

Veronica puts her hands on her hips and turns to Jareth with a quizzical expression. "And didn't you say that I told you I changed my mind or something?"

Jareth nods, adamant. "Yes. You came back after you left to meet your dad and you told me you were worried about me, and that if keeping me safe meant voting for Cassandra to be benched, you would do it."

She raises an eyebrow and shakes her head. "I definitely did not do that. I didn't come back after leaving this morning, not until just now."

Jareth squeezes his eyes shut and shakes his head in consternation. "What the heck is going on here? Are we all going crazy, seeing things that aren't real?"

A hard edge fixes to Tristan's jaw, and his bright blue eyes narrow over Brielle's shoulder. "No, I don't think we are. All this stuff started happening when *he* came around."

Brielle looks behind her in the direction of Tristan's glare —at Kerrim, who's sitting on the couch, watching them.

Tristan stalks past her to stand in front of Kerrim, and

they all follow. "What did you say your power is?" he asks Kerrim, crossing his arms over his chest.

Kerrim uncrosses his legs and stands, rising to the clear challenge in Tristan's voice. "As the Scorpio, I have the power to manipulate shadows, and to sense and manipulate the inhibitions of others."

"Brielle?" Tristan asks without turning away from Kerrim.

She knows what he's asking, and she doesn't like the turn this situation has taken. "If you're asking me whether or not Kerrim is lying, the answer is no. He's telling the truth."

"Just because the things he's saying are true doesn't mean he's not omitting anything," Tristan declares. "You haven't outright denied that you didn't have something to do with any of the confusing situations today."

"I wasn't aware I'd been accused of anything," Kerrim says, his expression unreadable.

"Then let me make it clear," Tristan says, taking a step closer to him. "Did you mess with Cassandra's inhibitions to make her kill Richard?"

"No, I didn't," Kerrim declares, looking past him to Brielle. "Did I, Brielle?"

Tristan does turn to her this time, and she shakes her head, sensing no lie.

Tristan's scowl deepens as he turns back to face Kerrim. "Do you have any other powers that we are not aware of?"

Kerrim shrugs. "I'm sure we all do. Though I may be more versed in our powers than the rest of you, I'm sure there are still things I don't know about my own limitations."

Tristan growls in agitation, stepping even closer, and Brielle can sense that a fight is imminent.

She moves between them. "That's enough, Tristan. Just because Kerrim happened to join us right when all these weird things started happening doesn't mean he's the cause of any of it. He's a Zodiac, the same as the rest of us. He's part of our team, and I think we've had enough arguing in our group today to last a lifetime. Not trusting each other is what got us all into this mess. So can we please try to trust each other?"

The look on Tristan's face makes it clear that trusting—specifically Kerrim—is not on his to-do list.

The argument is far from over.

26

TRISTAN

T ristan steps around Brielle, keeping his gaze lasered on Kerrim.

On the one guy who conveniently appeared right before all this started.

"Did you want to answer a question directly?" he challenges.

Kerrim's eyes narrow ever so slightly, and Tristan wonders if the others can even see it. Then again, no one has realized what a slimy player this guy is, Zodiac or not. "It's interesting that you think I'm being evasive. You'd like the others to think that, wouldn't you?"

The anger already heating every inch of Tristan's skin increases by a few hundred degrees. "Says the guy who just avoided answering." He steps closer. "Again."

Kerrim doesn't back down, and a flash of satisfaction spears through Tristan when he registers an echo of fury in the guy's dark eyes. "How about we get to the heart of this?" Kerrim challenges.

"Unlike you, I'm all for the truth," Tristan snaps back.

"Then maybe it's time you admit this is all because you're jealous." Kerrim shrinks the distance between them and jabs his finger into Tristan's chest. "You can't handle that I'm with Brielle."

Hurt is a white-hot blade as it slices through the crimson cloud of anger. And the gaping gash exposes what's beneath. Corrosive, green jealousy. Tristan hates seeing Brielle with Kerrim. It's eating him alive.

But that's not what this is about. Tristan knocks Kerrim's hand away. "That's probably because you've never given her a straight answer either," he snarls.

Kerrim's nostrils flare. "Are you doubting her judgment? Again?"

Fury is weaving a tight cocoon around Tristan. Everything that's gone wrong happened after Kerrim arrived. And he needs the others to see that.

He needs Brielle to see that.

"Answer the question, Kerrim. Were you there when Richard was killed?" Tristan asks, watching him closely. Any flicker of his dark gaze, any tightening of his features, and he'll see it.

Not that he needs to. Brielle will sense the lie if Kerrim doesn't answer truthfully. And she'll finally realize exactly how wrong he is for her.

Kerrim's face does change. It twists with his own heated anger. He shoves Tristan in the chest. "Answer this, Tristan. What sort of leader are you?" He shoves him again. "Considering you can't stop your emotions from clouding your judgment."

The barb hits so deep and so fast, that Tristan's moved before he's realized it. Pain and fury power his fist as it arcs towards Kerrim's face. The promise of connecting with the prick's jaw is the only way to assuage them.

Except Kerrim leans away as he swiftly blocks the strike, and the fist that was acting like a homing missile to his face whooshes past his nose. The momentum tugs Tristan off balance and he stumbles forward just as Kerrim slices his elbow upward.

Brielle's cry echoes behind him. "Stop it!"

But this has been coming from the moment Kerrim unsettled and undermined the unity of the Zodiacs. By making Brielle his mark.

Tristan weaves around the strike aiming to smash his nose, and it glances off his cheek. Ignoring the shocking pain because the guy's bones seem to be molded of steel, he speeds up his downward momentum and turns it into a spin. His head arcs low as his leg swipes high. There's a very satisfying click as it connects with Kerrim's jaw.

Kerrim stumbles backward, the blow rippling through his body, but he recovers quickly. His lip curls on a growl as he moves to attack again.

Tristan welcomes the rush of adrenaline. He can't wait to annihilate this guy.

But then Brielle slips between them again. "Stop it," she shouts. "Stop it!"

Tristan rears back, trying to reign in the fury and stumbling a little. Kerrim manages to do it much quicker. He leaps back, opening his hands as if he's still being attacked.

"You're acting like…like meatheads!" she cries, her head swiveling between the two of them.

Tristan finds he's panting as he glares at Kerrim. "You did this on purpose," he growls, realization hitting him just as hard as the elbow did. "You baited me into a fight!"

Brielle pushes herself into his line of sight, blocking Tristan's view of Kerrim. "Are you even listening? We're Zodiacs! Protectors of the Universe! How can we do that when we're trying to beat each other to a pulp!"

Tristan shakes his head. Although the anger has abated, the need to prove he's right is stronger than ever. "Don't you see?" he cries. "He didn't answer the question!" Kerrim never denied he had anything to do with Richard's death, or any of the other pieces of the puzzle that are missing.

Brielle's shoulders slump as disappointment fills her eyes. She steps back, as if she needs distance from him. "Neither did you," she says quietly.

Answer this, Tristan. What sort of leader are you?

Tristan reels back, those words ricocheting through him. He opens his mouth to defend himself, but then a movement catches in his periphery. Someone just shifted their weight. Everyone else seems frozen.

Tristan scans the room, seeing a circle of horrified eyes. Jareth. Veronica. Cassandra. Logan. Ada. Eric. Shreya.

They just witnessed Tristan physically fighting another Zodiac. Shame sweeps through him, far hotter and more caustic than the anger that was powering him a minute ago.

They're all witnessing their leader lose it.

Sweet Pitch, he's just let everyone down, Brielle most of all.

He spins on his heel, his gaze brushing over Kerrim. The one at the heart of all of this. The prick doesn't look away, rubbing his jaw as if it hurts. Subtly playing the victim.

Before he can add to the actions-he-regrets pile, Tristan spins on his heel. He needs to get out of here. He needs to figure out how to untangle this whole freaking mess.

And he needs to find proof Kerrim is at the heart of it.

The silence presses in as Tristan stalks to the door, feeling like a weight is pressing on his chest. Or maybe that's his guilt. And self-loathing. And deep, crippling doubt. The Zodiac's don't need to see that, too.

"Ah, Tristan?"

He almost considers not responding to Shreya, but something in her voice stops him. Shreya's never sounded so…serious.

He turns around to find something glowing in her palm. It looks like a key.

She extends it, clearly alarmed. "Why is it doing that?"

27

SHREYA

The key in Shreya's palm is emanating a faint pale glue glow, and it warms her skin in a way that's not unpleasant or abrasive. It feels…comforting.

She'd been carrying it around with her in her pocket, considering it a sort of good luck charm seeing as she found it just before she learned she was a Zodiac. The spot on her upper thigh had begun to tingle as she watched the argument and resulting brawl at a distance, and the last thing she expected to find when she reached in to inspect it was it glowing like some magical trinket.

"What is it?" Tristan asks, seeming unsure as to what relevance this may have.

She shrugs. "I don't know. I found it the day I met all of you. I was hoping you would know."

Suddenly, all of their watches ding simultaneously, followed by Esther's voice in stereo. "Dark matter signature identified."

Acting as a unit, they all check their watches at the same time. There's a pair of coordinates on the screen of Shreya's watch, and she looks up at the others for a clue as to what they might mean.

"Whatever that key goes to must be what triggered the dark matter signature," Tristan concludes. "We need to get there ASAP."

Just then, he finally seems to notice the large, jacket-wrapped object Shreya's been holding in her other hand all this time. In all the commotion, he hadn't really looked at her, but now he can't seem to take his eyes off her.

"What is that?" He nods at it.

"I...er..." Shreya looks to Brielle, not sure how to go about their big reveal after everything that's just happened.

Brielle steps forward, taking the Staff from Shreya. "I was going to show this to all of you before I discovered the mayhem had broken loose." She removes her jacket to expose it.

The light from the recessed bulbs overhead glint off the shiny metal of its impressive, embellished head, and Tristan's mouth falls open as he sucks in a gasp.

"Is that...?" He can't seem to finish the question, his eyes glued to it and his mouth practically watering.

"The Staff," Brielle verifies with a nod.

"How did you—Where did you—When—?" he stammers, seemingly unable to decide on a line of questioning.

Brielle takes in a deep breath through her nose and squares her shoulders. "Solomon gave me the locations of all pieces, and Shreya and I tracked them down. I rushed it over here as soon as he put them all together."

His brows crease in the beginnings of an accusation. "You worked with Solomon again? After he stole the book from us?"

Brielle flinches at his rise in tone, but Shreya steps in to defend her. "Yes, she did. And she came prepared this time, knowing he couldn't be trusted. He wanted us to find the Staff so that he could destroy it, but Brielle chloroformed him before he could get his hands on it. She was kinda awesome, actually."

The crease moves from between his eyebrows to his forehead as his eyes widen in admiration. "Wow. But still, why didn't you tell us about it? We could have all worked together to find the pieces."

Brielle keeps eye contact with him, and Shreya wonders if anyone else can see her sheer need to earn Tristan's approval. "Because after what happened with the book, I knew you would never trust him, and I couldn't pass up the chance to get the Staff. And...I needed to prove to you, to myself, that I could do it."

He frowns, and holy cow, does everyone else see how head over heels he is for her? Why don't they just hook up already? Seriously, Shreya could cut the sexual tension between them with a butter knife!

"I think it's time you start giving your team members a little more credit," Kerrim remarks, and Tristan's eyes narrow to slits as they flicker in his direction, but he doesn't turn to acknowledge him any further than that.

"May I?" he asks, holding his hands out toward the artifact.

Shreya nods, but Brielle quickly steps in and takes it. "Right now, we need to hide it. There's a change in dark matter to check out."

"I agree," Ada says. "As awesome as this is, we should go investigate the signature before it disappears."

"Right," Tristan says, lowering his hand and clearly trying to hide his disappointment. "We'll put this under our tightest security, then go check out the ping. But from now on, everyone," he looks around from face-to-face, "we have to start working as a team. No more secrets, no more solo missions. We have to trust each other or this will never work."

They all nod, and Brielle goes into the secret room to hide the Staff, Shreya assumes in some hi-tech alien vault made out of liquid metal like something out of a Terminator movie.

"Alright, let's go," Tristan announces when Brielle returns, leading the way to the garage door.

They all follow. Tristan, Brielle and Shreya climb into the front seat of Tristan's truck, and Ada, Eric and Kerrim hop into its bed while Cassandra, Logan, Veronica and Jareth squeeze into Jareth's little yellow bug. Shreya would've assumed they'd all be driving super cool Humvees or something like that, but these vehicles do seem way more low profile.

Shreya can't help but find it odd that Brielle opts to sit next to Tristan rather than with Kerrim in the back. Isn't she with Kerrim? And yet she so clearly is in love with Tristan. Shreya decides she really needs to get the back story on their weird love-hate thing. As they drive to the location of the coordinates, she wants to ask, but her little inner compass tells her it would be a bad idea. There's no way either of them is going to be honest in front of the other about their feelings, that much has been made crystal clear.

Tristan's GPS leads them way out of town, past all the farmland and into a thick wood. Shreya's never seen this part of New York. She'd always assumed the area was nothing but packed in apartments and over-compensating skyscrapers, so it's refreshing to see something untouched.

"Could this be a trap?" Brielle asks, breaking the long, brittle silence.

"I always assume everything is a trap," Tristan says. "But I don't think so." He looks at the key still firmly gripped in Shreya's hand. "That looks like alien tech. It has the same symbols as the book and the Staff. I think we're about to find something of ours."

"I hope so," Brielle says, the hope that never seems far away making her smile.

They slow to a stop in an area that's so tight with trees, they really can't go any farther.

"This is it," Tristan says, turning off the ignition and stepping out of the truck. "Everyone, look around," he says as they all get out.

Shreya wanders in a direction to the left of where they've parked, breathing the fresh scents of pine and wet dirt. She hasn't gone hiking in way too long. She might come back here after this little adventure for a good walk. There's nothing more freeing, more satisfying to her than just exploring something new and marveling at whatever she finds.

As she pushes through a couple of tall shrubs, something white catches in her periphery. She turns that way and pulls back a group of tall bushy branches, and what she sees has her eyes nearly popping out of her head.

"Guys, you'd better come check this out!" she calls with unbridled glee.

Fallen leaves crunch behind her in stereo as everyone gathers around.

"What is it?" Shreya asks, unable to stop staring at it.

Tristan is the one who answers, sounding surprised. "It's a pod."

TRISTAN

Disbelief holds Tristan immobile for long seconds. Another pod? Just sitting like this in the forest? The other Zodiacs fan out, varying shades of the same shock coloring their faces.

Then Tristan notes something. "It's not like the pods we arrived in."

Brielle glances at him. "Why would you say that?"

"It's smaller than the others," he says, eyes roaming over its oval smoothness, noting the little, oddly shaped divots scattered along a central line. "And these strange shapes weren't on the others."

"Plus Esther would've scanned this area multiple times," adds Ada.

Eric nods. "This one arrived fairly recently."

"So it just landed? From outer space?" breathes Shreya. "That's so cool."

Jareth's brows twitch. "It means we don't know what's in it."

Tristan nods, having considered that himself. They have

no idea who sent this or why. "Esther. Can you detect anything?"

"No," she says through their watches. "The changes in dark matter have stopped. The pod is currently neutral."

Logan rubs his chin. "Chardis may have sent this."

"Or it could be a message for us," Cassandra says, excitement making her bounce on her toes.

Tristan slowly circles it. "Either way, there's no clear way in."

"I think this may do that." Everyone turns to Shreya to see her palm extended, the key sitting on it is glowing the brightest it has so far. She grins. "I knew it was special the moment I saw it."

And Tristan doubts it could've fallen into the lap of anyone but Shreya. Her good luck powers are impressive. And another part of the Zodiac puzzle that will mean they can defeat Chardis when the time comes.

Unless that time is now.

"Shreya wouldn't have found it if this wasn't a good thing?" Brielle offers.

Tristan inclines his head, admitting that makes sense. Involuntarily, his gaze shifts to Kerrim, the one Zodiac who hasn't spoken. The guy simply stares back, as if his very existence is a challenge. Tristan looks away, pushing away the animosity that climbs up his throat like a black spider. He doesn't trust Kerrim, but he'll have to deal with that later.

An unexpected pod has dropped into the forest.

And they have the key to open it.

Shreya bounces a little. "I say we open it. It could be from one of our home planets."

Eric shifts his weight, the skin around his eyes tightening. "Maybe it's from Aqua."

Tristan's heart clenches. It was devastating to watch Aqua be destroyed, but for Eric most of all. The people he'd been searching for all his life were on that planet. All they can do is hope the message that they escaped to the Ark is true.

"Suit up, Zodiacs," says Tristan, and the word "Akash" echoes around him. He nods at Shreya. "See what the key does if you bring it closer."

Her eyes light up in her pixie face a second before her visor encases her face. She takes a tentative step closer to the pod. "Ooh, it's getting warmer."

Not only that, the key lifts from her palm, hovering and trembling an inch above it.

Tristan can feel the Zodiacs collectively holding their breath. "Be ready for anything," he tells them in a low voice.

Shreya, now encased in a sunny yellow suit, walks closer to the pod. With each inch, the key hovers higher and brighter, the pale blue light progressively changing until it's the same white as the pod. Suddenly, shards of light spear out from its center as it fractures into several parts. Each piece, now uneven and oddly shaped, shoots toward the small depressions on the surface of the pod.

"It wasn't just one key," gasps Shreya. "It was lots of keys!"

"I wonder if whoever sent this shaped it into something we would recognize on Earth," Ada murmurs thoughtfully.

Tristan can see the logic. All those strange, small parts wouldn't have resembled anything familiar. The pieces slot into the hollows, blending and disappearing to create a seamless surface over the pod.

"Get ready," he warns, his hands forming into fists.

All that happens is the outline of a hand appears on the rounded nose of the pod, pulsing softly. Waiting for someone to press their palm on it. So much for keeping their distance... Deciding that needs to be him, Tristan takes a step forward.

"Tristan!" Brielle's cry has adrenalin instantly spiking through his veins. He looks up to find her pointing behind him. Without thinking, he spins and drops, throwing out a strike.

His punch collides with a chest at the same time the sounds of battle break out in the forest.

"Skins!" Logan shouts.

"They must've traced the changes in dark matter, too," Eric grunts, executing a flying kick a second later. His foot plows into a Skin, propelling the man into a tree trunk.

"Don't let them get to the pod!" Tristan cries, leaping high and then slamming his forearms down on the shoulders of the nearest Skin. The guy crumples like he was just hit by a jackhammer.

The Zodiacs instantly move to form a protective circle around the pod as dozens of Skins materialize from the forest in every direction. Cassandra shoots a fireball, obliterating two. Eric drops another three, and Ada electrocutes them as they writhe in pain. Logan and Jareth stay close to Shreya, Jareth creating snakes and spiders and fire as Logan amplifies the Skin's instinctive flashes of fear. It allows their latest addition to triumphantly get some strikes in, despite her lack of training. Even Kerrim is fighting with quite a bit of skill, not seeming to need his powers as he knocks Skin after Skin down.

Tristan goes to join them only for a Skin to drop down from the branches above, landing straight in front of him. "Get the Gemini!" he shouts and several more Skins appear in front of him, blocking his path to the pod.

"Tristan!" Brielle cries.

"No, let them," he says, taking a few steps backward as several Skins converge on him. "It's better they keep their focus on me."

Rather than the pod.

He quickly becomes a flurry of punches and kicks and blocks, especially when more Skins materialize as if they're cloning themselves on the spot. Tristan ducks and weaves and strikes, noting that the other Zodiacs are fighting just as hard, but managing to keep the Skins away from the pod.

Three Skins close in on Tristan, looking bigger than the others as they block his line of sight. One glances over Tristan's shoulder, a sneer contorting his face as he nods imperceptibly.

"I'm not falling for that," mutters Tristan as he kicks backward, keeping his gaze on the attackers in front of him. Just as he suspected, his leg arcs through nothing but air.

But the change of focus is all the Skins need. Probably all they were wanting. They contract, one dropping low to sweep at Tristan's remaining leg. He leaps to avoid it, but once again, it's what the Skins wanted. The next one jumps and slams an elbow in Tristan's face. The third spins and powers his foot into Tristan's chest.

He's propelled backward so fast, it actually hurts when he slams into the tree trunk, despite his suit. But even as he's crumpling, Tristan's already planning on getting back up. He's taken down more Skins than three before. And he has no intention of letting them get to the pod first.

Except they have other plans.

The third Skin turns and runs straight for the pod. The second leaps forward, the thirst for blood tightening his features as Tristan tries to still his swimming head.

"Mild concussion detected," comes Esther's voice. "Retreat recommended."

"Like pitch," Tristan mutters as he braces himself for the Skin coming at him.

He lifts his head in time to see the first one pull out a gun. One that's not from Earth.

"One Gemini down," the Skin snarls. "Then the rest of you Zodiac scum will crumble."

The Skin who looks like he intends on fulfilling that

promise with his bare hands barrels into Tristan, slamming him into the tree a second time, eliciting a soft groan. The Skin rains punches down on him and although Tristan still manages to block most of them, a few get past his defenses. Each one rattles his brain a little more.

"Tristan!"

Brielle's voice reaches through their comms. How is it that she's always the first to notice he's in trouble?

"The pod," he groans. "Don't let them get to it."

Even as the words tumble past his lips, Tristan registers the Skin who made a run for it angle toward a gap in the Zodiacs. Simultaneously, the Skin with the gun lifts it and aims it at him. Alarm rings through Tristan's mind along with the pain, and he tries to stand up. A punch that feels like a battering ram plows into his jaw.

"Consciousness at twenty-seven percent," says Esther. "I repeat, retreat recommended."

Except it's too late. Tristan's legs feel a mile away. Even his arms are difficult to place right now. And he's staring down the barrel of an alien weapon.

A movement beyond the Skin catches Tristan's attention. The Skin is almost at the pod, but it's not that. Kerrim is running straight at him. He can stop him!

But Kerrim runs straight past the Skin. He leaps high, sailing through the air with impressive speed, and lands beside the Skin with the gun. A strike to his lower back has him arching, a second to his throat and he collapses. Two strides and he hauls the Skin standing over Tristan away, throwing him into a nearby stand of rocks. The man falls to the ground, silent.

Kerrim stands over Tristan and extends his hand. Tristan takes it, still trying to comprehend what just happened.

"Thanks," he says gruffly as Kerrim pulls him up.

"Any Zodiac would've done the same," Kerrim says mildly.

Except Kerrim is the one Zodiac Tristan couldn't bring himself to trust. Seems that sentiment was misplaced. The Scorpio just saved his life.

"Get away from it!" shouts Cassandra.

Tristan and Kerrim look up in time to see her break into a run. Ignoring her, the Skin reaches the pod and reaches out, slamming his hand down on the softly glowing outline.

The effect is instantaneous.

The pod's surface fractures, veins of fiery red zigzagging across it. A faint *click* sounds.

"Run!" Tristan shouts. "It's going to—"

The pod explodes, becoming a fireball in the space of a blink. Blinding white light blazes, forcing Tristan to close his eyes as a boom of energy knocks him back a step.

Breathing hard, he slowly lowers the arm he'd raised to protect his face, unsure whether it's over. The explosion was practically silent. But the pod is gone, the Earth it was resting on a scorched gray. Tristan glances around frantically. The Skin who tried to open it has been thrown back several feet. He lies, lifeless, beside a shrub, flames nibbling at the edges of his clothes. The remaining Skins are gone. Cowards.

"Is everyone okay?" Tristan calls.

"Yes," says Jareth, also lowering his arms.

"Fine," Ada and Eric say simultaneously, moving to hold each other.

"Sure am," Shreya says, somehow still managing to sound chirpy as she inspects her suit.

"My ass is bruised," mutters Cassandra, dusting it off.

"I'll help you with that," quips Logan.

Tristan's eyes fall on the one Zodiac he needs to hear a yes from the most. Brielle's closer than he expected, as if she too, was coming to his aid. "Are you okay?" she asks.

He finds himself almost smiling but then he glances at Kerrim standing next to him. "Yeah. I am."

Brielle's shoulders relax, and although Tristan can't see her face behind her visor, he suspects she's smiling, too. Probably because Kerrim saved his ass.

Tristan turns his focus back to the singed grass that once held the pod, conscious it came at a price. If the pod held a message for them, they'll never know.

It just self-destructed.

Probably because a Skin tried to open it.

29

BRIELLE

The lights in the house are on when Brielle rides up on her bike. As nice as it is to have Frank home again after his wrongful incarceration, she's not exactly in the mood to talk. Today has been a very long, eventful day—some great, some not so great—and all she wants to do is get into her bed and crash. She can't even think about eating, and food is her favorite thing in the whole world.

When she walks in the kitchen door after locking up her bike in the garage, she finds the kitchen is empty, and there are no smells to suggest Bea prepared any food. That's good. Bea and Frank need their time together and probably don't want to waste any of it being apart so that she can cook. It also means that, hopefully, Brielle can escape to her room and enjoy some undisturbed rest.

She turns off the kitchen light and heads down the hall, practically floating on the need to crawl into bed. But just as her hand reaches the doorknob, Bea emerges from her room, a tenuous smile on her face.

"Did you have a good day, sweetheart?" she asks.

Brielle tries to wake up her features so she doesn't look so exhausted. Whatever Bea needs from her, she owes it to her to show up for it as much as possible. "Eh, as good as it could be, I guess."

Bea nods, a nervous energy humming from her as she clearly struggles to express or contain whatever's going through her mind.

"What's up?" Brielle asks, curiosity—and concern—rousing her senses. Did something happen with Frank's charges? Is there a problem with the house or the bills? A slurry of possible troubles snowball into a knot of anxiety inside her as she waits for Bea to respond.

Bea rubs the back of her jeans with her hands. "Uh, I have something…rather difficult to talk to you about." She waves one of her hands toward Brielle's door. "Can we sit on your bed and talk for a bit?"

Brielle's throat tightens as she nods and opens her door, anticipation coiling her guts as she wonders what this could possibly be about.

Bea sits on the edge of the bed and pats the spot next to her, inviting Brielle to join her, which she does. Bea takes in a shaky breath, looking down at the floor.

"This is going to be hard for me to say, and even harder for you to hear. But I'm just going to come out with it." Bea looks up to meet Brielle's cautious gaze. "Frank and I know the truth. We always have, from the very beginning."

Brielle's throat constricts even tighter, her pulse pounding in her temples. She manages to squeak out, "Truth?"

Bea nods once. "That you're a Zodiac Guardian, the Libra to be precise."

Brielle can actually feel all the color drain from her face, and her skin feels so cold from the lack of blood that it almost burns. Her mind is spinning with so much panic, dread and confusion that she can't form words into a response. She just sits there like a statue as her insides bounce around like ping-pong balls in an empty room.

Bea places her hand over one of Brielle's that's resting on her lap, and Brielle instinctively twitches, which causes Bea to withdraw and tuck both her hands between her legs. Her expression is clearly one of hurt, but Brielle can't bring herself to comfort her. She doesn't even know if she can trust her. Has this whole adoption been a lie?

"We're so sorry for keeping this from you," Bea says, her voice strained. "We have been Zodiac sympathizers for years, and when Alden came to us—"

"Alden came to you?" The words rush out of Brielle's mouth like an accusation, hi-pitched and fast.

Bea winces at the tone of Brielle's voice, but continues. "Yes, we'd worked with him closely on extra-terrestrial matters for a long time, just trying to do whatever we could to help. He came to us a few months ago and told us about you. That you were a wonderful, intelligent, sweet girl in need of a loving home, and protection." She wipes at the corner of her eye, the moisture on her finger catching the light from Brielle's bedside lamp as she replaces her hand between her knees. "We hoped that we could give you that."

Brielle swallows, trying to contain her emotions from spilling out like molten lava. "So...that's the only reason you adopted me? Do you even...*like* me?"

Bea's reaction is immediate. "Oh, yes, of course, honey! We *love* you!" She wraps Brielle into a motherly hug before she can stop herself, but Brielle can't seem to reciprocate. She doesn't know how to feel. "We only ever wanted to give you and the Zodiacs your best chance of succeeding in this war. But we never imagined that you would fit so perfectly into the hole in our hearts. You're the daughter we always dreamed of but never thought we could have. Truly. And even if you hate us now, we will still always love you and be here for you with open arms."

"I—I don't hate you," Brielle says slowly, unmoving in Bea's embrace. "I'm just… This is a lot to handle."

Bea finally lets her go and backs up a few inches. "Of course. Yes. Of course." Brielle's never seen her so flustered, not even when Frank was in prison.

Brielle furrows her brow. "Why are you telling me this now? After all this time. Why now?"

"Right." Bea inhales sharply. "We, er, we know you have the Staff."

Shock, intricately woven with a thousand other emotions, spears through Brielle's chest like an arrow. "How could you possibly know that?"

"Solomon came here looking for it," Bea replies sheepishly. "When he gave us the book, we didn't know he was going to go after the Staff, or that he was going to use you to get it."

"You've been working with Solomon?" Betrayal seeps from the metaphorical wound in her chest like warm blood. She doesn't know these people at all.

"We knew him through Alden," Bea says defensively. "Although his intentions are often selfish, he is a rather resourceful man and has proven invaluable at acquiring what's needed to win this war."

Shaking her head, Brielle stands up and combs her fingers through her hair, feeling like she's going to explode from all these surprises.

"I hate to ask you this, but where is the Staff?" Bea asks tentatively. "We need to hide it to make absolutely certain no one will ever find it."

Brielle spins on Bea, anger climbing over her other warring emotions for the spotlight. "It's already well hidden."

"Are you sure?" Bea presses. "We can't allow it to fall back into Chardis's hands."

Brielle's eyes narrow, both out of anger and curiosity. "Back? What do you mean?"

"The Staff used to belong to Chardis, but Alden stole it and brought it with him here to Earth," Bea explains. "Chardis's son will stop at nothing to retrieve it for his father. If it gets put together, its power will call to him. We can't let him find it."

"Wait, Chardis has a son?" She thought Chardis was more of a Universal entity, not a real person. That he only took the form of a person to deal with others.

"Yes, and we're quite certain he's already here."

Brielle's heart slams against her ribcage. She needs to warn Tristan. "We'll make sure he never gets anywhere near it."

She shoots to her feet, admitting to herself that she's actually relieved to be heading back to HQ. Turns out there were more bombshells at home than there.

She's just reached the door when Bea calls out her name. She stands slowly, uncertainty flashing across her features. "We really do love you, Brielle. I hope you can forgive us for lying to you for so long."

Brielle hesitates. Her heart hurts. Her mind is a whirl. She wants to give this woman who's been the only mother she's known the reassurance she's seeking, but it's too soon.

"I'll talk to Tristan and the others, then come home," she says quietly, slipping out of her room.

Right now, she's going to focus on the Staff.

And making sure it doesn't end up in the wrong hands.

30

TRISTAN

Tristan paces the length of HQ as he waits for Brielle to turn up. She said there's something important they need to discuss. All the other Zodiacs are scattered around the room. He can practically see the scenes from the forest playing behind their preoccupied gazes. Shreya is chewing her lip. Cassandra's right leg is bouncing like a spring on speed. Jareth is rubbing his temples. Logan is staring at his thumb as it massages the opposite palm.

Only one person is actually looking somewhere but down, and that's Kerrim. He's watching Tristan pace, his arms crossed. Tristan wonders if it's a defensive gesture or if he's just trying to show off his biceps.

He stops, realizing exactly where his thoughts went. His default with Kerrim has always been distrustful. Harsh. And it turns out, unfair. Tristan suppresses a sigh, not liking the other truth that now sits beside the knowledge the pod is gone. His jealousy clouded his judgment.

"Thanks for saving me back there," he says, trying to not sound like he's struggling to let go of the grudge, but not quite succeeding.

Kerrim shrugs a shoulder, his arms loosening across his chest. "I don't understand why those Skins have it in for you," he says dryly.

Tristan arches a brow. "Even though you disobeyed orders."

"You're welcome," Kerrim says with a rather regal incline of his head.

Tristan snorts and shakes his head. A glance passes between them. An understanding. A truce.

A way forward as two Zodiacs fighting for the same end —defeating Chardis.

"Hey, at least we have the Staff," Shreya pipes up, seeming to want to make the most of the easing tension.

"Yeah, that's something," Tristan admits. Today wasn't a total loss. "The Staff is important. I can feel it."

"Zodiacs," comes Esther's voice. "I have something to report."

Tristan resists the urge to rub the bridge of his nose. He's not sure he can cope with more bad news. "Yes, Esth—"

Rapid footsteps sound down the stairs and Brielle appears in the doorway. The usual jolt of sunshine through his veins at seeing her is quickly tempered by the expression on her face. "Brielle? Is everything okay?"

She shakes her head, swallows, then twists her hands together. The trio of gestures instantly puts Tristan on edge. Behind him, Jareth pushes to his feet, his chair rolling a few inches over the floor. "What is it?"

"The Staff," she chokes. "It's gone."

Shock explodes through Tristan. "What?"

"It—it's not where we left it. I've looked everywhere. It's gone."

Tristan's lost the ability to move. The Staff can't be gone! Disbelief has him so firmly in its clutches that it's almost hard to breathe. Even the edges of his vision darken. Maybe his mind is trying to shut down, hoping to reboot and today would've never happened.

Except the black keeps creeping in, like ink blotches spreading across parchment. Tristan realizes it's not shock or shutdown. It's a vision.

"Tristan?"

But then Brielle's gone. So is HQ, right along with reality.

Tristan finds himself in a wide, brightly lit corridor, but not one he's ever seen before. Smooth white lines the walls and ceiling, reminding him of the pods they arrived in. Every edge is a curve and despite the pale coloring, everything shines as if it's metal. Long windows stretch down one side, and he blinks when he registers what's on the other side. Space. Stars. A distant sun.

Executing a slow turn, Tristan realizes where he is. The Ark!

As he returns to his original position, two things catch his attention. A crowd of people running toward him, panicking and screaming. And a terrifying ship lowering into view beyond the window. White flares from the thick guns protruding at its sides, shooting explosions of light that head straight for the Ark.

And the people inside it.

A blast tears through the side of the Ark. People are thrown through the air, their bodies instantly mangled and maimed. Devastated and dismembered. Blood paints the smooth, white walls. Screams are drowned out by explosions, then cut off by a powerful rush of air. The side of the Ark where the blast hit is imploding. The rest of the refuge will be next.

Tristan doubles over, devastated by the death and destruction. "No," he moans.

The vision fades as if his denial just banished it. He straightens to find he's back in the spotless corridor, the peaceful vista of space outside the window. Tristan walks to it, even though there's nothing he can do but watch. All he can hope is that the first vision is the one they never want to come true.

The deadly ship once more drops into view. This time Tristan notes the lines of the hulking black mass are edged in red. The colors of death and blood. He has no doubt it's one of Chardis's and it's probably not the only ship out there. The Ark would be surrounded. The blast is about to come any second. He finds himself holding his breath, not wanting to endure watching this all over again.

Just like before, there's a blast of light, but this time it's closer, as if it came from the Ark. A heartbeat later, Chardis's ship violently explodes, blinding light forcing Tristan to close his eyes. Even behind his eyelids, it feels like it sears his retinas.

He opens them, though, wanting to see the aftermath, only to find himself back in HQ. The well-lit room suddenly feels overcast compared to the brightness of the explosion he just witnessed.

Brielle steps into his line of view. "What did you see?"

It takes a few seconds to find his voice. "The Ark." A few gasps come from the other Zodiacs. "It was being attacked by Chardis."

Brielle frowns. "He destroys it in one of the visions, doesn't he?"

Tristan nods, glad for her perceptiveness. It's going to take him a few minutes before he can describe the grisly scenes he just witnessed.

Her face softens. "And in the second it's fine?"

He nods again, not surprised that she finds the ray of hope in the dark images still painting his mind. "Yeah. The ship and everyone on it survive."

"This won't be like the Aquarius planet," she says resolutely. "We'll make sure that vision is the true vision."

His thundering heart rate slows a little. The band around his chest eases. Of course it's Brielle that has this effect on him. The one person he can't be with…

"Have you sufficiently recovered, Tristan?" Esther asks through the speakers, having probably picked up on his lowered blood pressure.

He braces himself, realizing today isn't a day where he gets a break. "Yep, never better," he bites out.

"Excellent, because I still have the report to convey."

"Esther," Ada says, almost looking apologetic for this ultra-efficient AI she created. "Maybe—"

"It's fine," says Tristan, let's-get-this-done-with heavy in his tone.

"I was able to briefly connect to the pod's mainframe once the pieces of the key unlocked it," Esther says, still all business. "There was a message. About the Ark."

Tristan takes a step toward the nearest speaker and waits. He sighs when there's nothing but silence. "I'm all ears, Esther."

"That's not biologically possible."

"Continue, Esther," he says, once more gritting his teeth.

"It's from a lifeform on the Ark. It was in Aquarian, but I have the capability to translate it. I'll project it on the main screen."

The large screen on the wall fills with the image of a beautiful young woman. Midnight hair with highlights of luminescent blue flows over her shoulders, framing a delicate face. "I send this message from the Ark, a refuge for all those escaping the trail of destruction Chardis is unleashing across the Universe," she says, clasping her hands. The other Zodiacs move in around Tristan, watching with the same rapt attention he is. "We thought we were safe until we discovered a spy among us."

Brielle stiffens and Tristan instinctively clasps her hand, wanting to give reassurance as much as receive it. The woman before them is holding herself with regal stoicism, but it's obvious from the tight lines of her face she's worried. Probably scared. Brielle's hand tightens around his, and the sensation echoes somewhere in his chest.

"The spy has been killed," says the young woman, and Tristan senses some movement to his right. Kerrim just crossed his arms. "But we don't know how much he knew, or what he told Chardis. The Ark is in danger. We need help."

The recording cuts out, leaving the screen blank and black, and Tristan tries not to feel like it's an omen after what he just saw in his vision.

He glances at Kerrim, now glad they've reached a truce. The Staff will have to wait. Any differences or disagreements have to end. The visions and now the recording prove exactly how real the Ark is. That there are hundreds, maybe thousands of lives under threat.

Failure isn't an option.

Tristan releases Brielle's hand and turns, his gaze weighing on each Zodiac in turn. "No more arguments or accusations or distrust." The Zodiacs must unite, now more than ever. "We need to save the Ark."

Nothing has ever felt as good as cuddling against Logan's chest does right now, especially after the hellacious few days she's had.

They're in her bed in her room at Tristan's house. She supposes she should start calling it her house, but it doesn't feel like home. Honestly, nothing ever has. Not when she was still Richard's daughter, not when she was staying with Brielle, and certainly not back at the orphanage. It would be nice to have something that was just hers, outright. But for now, being in Logan's arms is the closest thing to home she could hope for.

"What do you think really happened to your dad?" Logan asks softly, gently running his fingertips up and down her bare arm.

She sighs. "I don't know. I've been mulling it over and over in my head, and I don't care what anyone else says they saw or what they think, I know I didn't do it." She picks a piece of lint off his t-shirt. "But I guess I owe a debt of gratitude to whatever Cassandra really did kill him. He's out of my life forever now and that's all I care about."

"What I don't get is why someone would try to frame you?" he muses. "Let alone how they could pull off looking like you and using your powers."

"Probably the same reason Jareth thought Veronica joined his side of the argument, and why Ada and Eric were having a lovers' spat," she says. "Someone is trying to make us fight each other so we're not fighting the real villain."

"Do you..." He falters, sighing through his nose for a moment. "Do you think Kerrim really could've had anything to do with it? Tristan did have some good points. And Kerrim never once openly denied the accusations. He just evaded. That's infiltration one-o-one. I've done it myself on assignments."

She shakes her head against his chest, too tired of all the back-and-forth to give it any further thought. "I think what Tristan said last is what we should do—stop doubting and mistrusting each other. Besides, if Kerrim really is up to no good, it's only a matter of time before he slips up. He's dating Brielle, for shit-sake. That girl is like a drug hound for lies. Honestly, if he really was the bad guy, he chose the absolute worst person to cozy up to."

Logan's touches stop. "Or the best. Making her trust him would make all of us trust him."

"Ugh, my head hurts too much to think about this anymore," she grouses. "Can we just cuddle?"

Logan squeezes his arm around her. "Maybe I can make your head stop hurting." His voice has that sultry tone to it that instantly makes Cassandra's insides heat deliciously.

She looks up at him with a playful grin. "Maybe you can."

He leans down to kiss her, but "Confident" by Demi Lovato blaring from her phone on the nightstand makes them both jump.

"Ugh," she complains as she grabs the phone, ready to silence it. But the caller ID makes her pause.

Sinclair Holdings.

Instantly, she sits up to answer it. "Hello?"

"Yes, is this Cassandra Sinclair?" a male voice on the other line asks.

"This is," she replies curiously.

"My name is Charles Manchester," he offers. "First off, I'd like to express my deepest condolences on your father's passing."

She rolls her eyes.

"His death truly was a tragedy, and I can only imagine what you might be—"

"Yes, yes, tragic," she cuts him off. "Can I help you with something?"

He clears his throat. "Right. Yes, on the matter of his investment company, you—well—you've inherited it. He had no beneficiaries in his will, and your mother seems to have fled the country, so New York Law states that all legal holdings be passed down to next of kin, which is you. I've been assigned to contact you to see how you'd like to handle the management. Are you interested in selling the company? We can pay you handsomely."

Cassandra has to physically push her jaw back up to close it.

Sinclair Holdings is hers? Just like that?

This suddenly changes *everything!* She doesn't have to scrape by and mooch off Tristan's sympathy, or anyone else's. She can actually have something that is truly hers. A home. Finances. Whatever the hell she wants. She could sell the company and live like a queen.

Or—she can take it over and secure her future for life.

"Ms. Sinclair?" Charles prompts after a few seconds of her silence.

"Um, no, I do not wish to sell the company," she states with confidence. "I would like to take the position my father held, after the management team shows me the ropes, of course."

"Very well," Charles says, sounding slightly deflated. "In that case, I've been appointed as your liaison until the time that you reach legal age. Perhaps you can meet me tomorrow after school to go over the finer details."

"Sounds great!"

"Alright, I've put you on the books for three-thirty tomorrow afternoon," he says. "Have a good evening, Ms. Sinclair."

The line goes dead, and she slowly lowers the phone into her lap, staring at the wall.

"What was that about?" Logan asks behind her.

She turns to him with the biggest, most triumphant grin she's ever worn. "That was my father's company. It's mine now."

Watch out world, Ms. Sinclair is the new rising star!

BRIELLE

The stove-top clock in the kitchen reads nine-o-five when Brielle finally walks in the front door. This has been the longest day of her entire life, and she's way more ready for it to be over than she was when she got home the first time this evening.

Thankfully, Kerrim was nice enough to drive her home so she didn't have to ride her bike in the dark. She still doesn't know how to feel toward him. He saved Tristan's life earlier at the pod in the forest, and she's unfathomably grateful for that. But...it's only because she still has such powerful feelings for Tristan.

Is it fair to be with Kerrim, to give him false hope of any kind of future together, when she knows she'll always hold a candle for another guy? Of course, Kerrim has never pushed for them to be anything other than physical, and even then he doesn't ask for more than she's willing to give. He's never pressured her to go farther than she wants to go. But how long will it take him to get tired of waiting, to catch the way she looks at Tristan and walk away?

And when he does, will she even want to stop him?

She hangs her keys on the hook by the door and heads into the hallway to her room, but once again, Bea emerges before she can get to safety, and this time Frank comes with her.

"Can we talk to you for a moment?" Frank asks, gesturing a hand toward the living room.

Brielle swallows back a sigh. "Okay, sure." Are they about to drop another bomb shell? She doesn't even know how to tell them that the Staff has been stolen. Or is this because they already know?

She follows them into the living room and sits in the armchair as they take up the loveseat catty-corner to it. Her stomach clenches with apprehension, like a child preparing to be reprimanded by her parents for doing something she knows they know about. But at least now, she can be fully open and honest with them. She never liked keeping things from them.

"We know today has been a stressful day," Bea begins. "After dropping everything on you earlier, the last thing we want is to burden you further. But…something has just come up, and this conversation can't wait till morning."

"What is it?" Brielle asks through a thick throat.

Frank leans forward, resting his elbows on his knees and braiding his fingers. "Richard Sinclair is dead."

Brielle's brows hike in surprise. This is so not where she thought this conversation was going. She swallows. "Yes, I know. There's been some…controversy among us as to who killed him." Pitch, it feels good to be able to tell them things!

Bea nods, seeming to understand. Surely they knew that the circumstances of his death pointed to the Zodiacs, despite Tristan's best efforts to cover it up.

"Well, the thing is, Sinclair Holdings is currently without leadership in his absence," Frank continues. "As our companies recently merged, I hold quite a bit of stock and legal control in it." He takes Bea's hand and squeezes it. "We are planning to take over the company and run it the right way. And we'd like you to play a major role in the company's management."

Brielle's eyes widen in shock. "I—but—I'm only seventeen. I don't have any credentials, I haven't even taken any college courses."

Frank nods and puts his hands up to assuage her. "After everything that's happened, we want to show you that we love you. That we're family."

Bea nods, her face soft. "We want to do this together."

"And the great thing about this is that it will not only give you valuable experience for getting into a great university, but it will also ensure that your education is paid in full," Frank adds. "The company will handle the costs."

"I—this is—a lot," she manages to say, overwhelmed with shock and humility.

"And, best yet, we can give you a company car," Bea interjects with a smile. "No more trekking all over town on your bike."

Tears pool at Brielle's eyelids. "Wow. I don't know what to say."

Frank smiles. "Just say yes."

She nods several times in eagerness. "Okay. Yes."

Ready for the next installment in the Zodiac Guardians series? Check out ARIES ARMED!

ARIES ARMED

Twelve teens. One task.
Save the Universe.

Ethan was a child when his pod crashed to Earth. He's always known he's a Zodiac and that he must find the others. He's honed his powers as he's searched for them relentlessly.

Having seen Chardis's thirst for destruction firsthand when he destroyed his home planet, Ethan grew up on the Ark. Finally uniting with the Zodiacs means he can fight to save the thousands of vulnerable refugees the Ark holds. What's more, his desperate search is personal. His childhood sweetheart is aboard.

Except the Zodiacs are fracturing. Long held friendships and deep connections are being undermined and manipulated, and this threat is one that none of them have considered—a threat from within.

Will they find the Ark in time? Especially when Tristan has foreseen two visions. One where the Ark is saved. The other where it's destroyed and everyone on board is brutally killed.

Grab your copy HERE!

mybook.to/AquariusUndone

MORE EPIC ROMANCE TO FALL IN LOVE WITH!

ALSO BY TAMAR SLOAN

PRIME PROPHECY SERIES

KEEPERS OF THE GRAIL

KEEPERS OF THE CHALICE

KEEPERS OF THE LIGHT

KEEPERS OF EXCALIBUR

DESTINED DEMIGODS

ELEMENTAL GAMES

THE SOVEREIGN CODE

THE THAW CHRONICLES

ALSO BY TRICIA BARR

THE MATING GAMES

THE BOUND ONE SERIES

THE AMARANT SERIES

SHIFTER ACADEMY

HEAVENLY SINNERS

ABOUT THE AUTHORS

By day, Tricia is a full time mom to two beautiful girls and a wife/business partner to a handsome hard-working husband. By night—and nap times—she's a USA Today Best-selling Author of unique and thrilling teen and adult fantasies inspired by her vivid, somewhat creepy dreams and her own adventures around the world.

Tamar hasn't decided whether she's a psychologist who loves writing, or a writer with a lifelong fascination with psychology. She must've been someone pretty awesome in a previous life (past life regression indicates a Care Bear), because she gets to do both. When not reading, writing, or working with teens, Tamar can be found with her husband and two sons enjoying country life in their small slice of the Australian bush.